Ururu

Len

Oruru

The Silver Wing Bandits

Nahura

Eruru

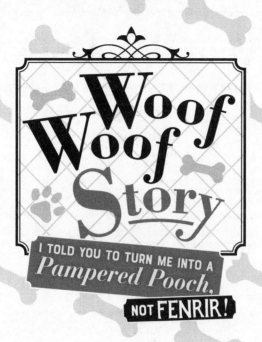

Woof Woof Story

I TOLD YOU TO TURN ME INTO A Pampered Pooch, NOT FENRIR!

3

Inumajin

ILLUSTRATION BY

Kochimo

YEN ON

NEW YORK

Woof Woof Story

I TOLD YOU TO TURN ME INTO A *Pampered Pooch,* NOT FENRIR!

Inumajin

VOLUME 3

Translation by Wesley O'Donnell
Cover art by Kochimo

WANWAN MONOGATARI Volume 3 -KANEMOCHI NO INU NI SHITETOWA ITTAGA, FENRIR NISHIROTOWA ITTENEE!-
© Inumajin, Kochimo 2018
First published in Japan in 2018 by KADOKAWA CORPORATION, Tokyo.
English translation rights arranged with KADOKAWA CORPORATION, Tokyo,
through TUTTLE-MORI AGENCY, INC., Tokyo.

English translation © 2019 by Yen Press, LLC

Yen On
150 West 30th Street, 19th Floor
New York, NY 10001

Visit us at yenpress.com

facebook.com/yenpress
twitter.com/yenpress

yenpress.tumblr.com
instagram.com/yenpress

First Yen On Edition: November 2019

Yen On is an imprint of Yen Press, LLC.
The Yen On name and logo are trademarks of Yen Press, LLC.

Library of Congress Cataloging-in-Publication Data
Names: Inumajin, author. | Kochimo, illustrator. | O'Donnell, Jennifer, translator.
Title: Woof woof story : I told you to turn me into a pampered pooch, not fenrir! / Inumajin ;
illustration by Kochimo ; translation by Jennifer O'Donnell ; cover art by Kochimo.
Other titles: Wanwan Monogatari. English | I told you to turn me into a pampered pooch, not fenrir!
Description: First Yen On edition. | New York, NY : Yen On, 2018–
Identifiers: LCCN 2018051028 | ISBN 9781975303181 (v. 1 : pbk.) | ISBN 9781975303204 (v. 2 : pbk.) |
ISBN 9781975358662 (v. 3 : pbk.)
Subjects: CYAC: Reincarnation—Fiction. | Wishes—Fiction. | Dogs—Fiction. | Fantasy.
Classification: LCC PZ7.1.I63 Wo 2018 | DDC [Fic]—dc23
LC record available at https://lccn.loc.gov/2018051028

ISBNs: 978-1-9753-5866-2 (paperback)
978-1-9753-8671-9 (ebook)

1 3 5 7 9 10 8 6 4 2

LSC-C

Printed in the United States of America

"Routa, feast your eyes upon this beautiful blade. This sword was forged by a direct descendant of the famous blacksmith Gengo Kisaragi."

"A-arwf? *(O-oh, is that right?)*"

What am I gonna do? It's only been three months since I was reborn in this world, but this is the most boring conversation I've been stuck in yet.

The deplorable beauty gushing over the sword is Zenobia. She's a knight who was invited to stay at the mansion and has since degenerated into a shameless freeloader.

Her hair is a fiery red, and her eyes burn with conviction. On the surface, she's the spitting image of a "cool beauty," the type popular with guys and ladies alike, but her personality is a big mess.

In a peaceful mansion with little else to do but train, she often seeks me out and forces me to play audience to her little demonstrations.

"Arwf... *(So sleepy...)*"

Before she woke me up, I was enjoying a nice nap under a tree in the garden, so I'm still a little groggy.

Her spirited weapon-fawning is going in one ear and right out the other.

I don't care all that much, so I'm mostly just sleepy.

"Hey, are you listening to me, Routa?"

"Arwf, arwf... *(Yeah, yeah, I'm listening...zzz...)*"

I respond while nodding off.

"It's just that this is such a work of art. When I think of everything that went into getting it to this point, I can't help but get a little fired up. Look at the pattern on the blade! If you don't use enough adamantium, this particular type of marking isn't even possible."

"Arwf... *(You don't say...)*"

Yawning a half-hearted reply, I scratch behind my ear with my hind leg. Ahhh, scratchy scratchy.

Even though I'm making it painfully obvious that I couldn't care less, Zenobia fails to take the hint.

She keeps going on about how wonderful her sword is, like a kid showing off their favorite toy.

"The carefully calculated curve of the blade, the delicate workmanship. No matter how you look at it, this is a masterpiece. Even you can tell, can't you?"

"Arwf, arwf... *(No, not really...)*"

Why would a former wage slave know anything about weapon quality? Talking to me about a sword is as pointless as talking about yesterday's weather.

Not that I care, but is it really okay for Zenobia to be out here talking to a dog by herself? Doesn't it make her look a little desperate?

Look, the maids are already staring through the window and gossiping.

"Hee-hee... It's so amazing... What an incredible sword..."

Zenobia doesn't notice and keeps gushing on and on about the intricacies of her sword.

She stares at the blade, entranced, as though it were made of gems. It's a new level of weird.

"It took a lot to get my hands on this sword. I followed rumors to several different weapon shops, and then it cost me three years of my adventurer's wages."

That's one hell of a purchase.

I don't know how much Zenobia earned back when she was an adventurer, but it seems like she was pretty famous, so I'm fairly sure that three years' worth of her wages was a hefty sum.

So here's a question. Why is she facing *me* while brandishing the sword?

"…You've beaten me before in our two previous matches."

She calls them *matches*, but what she's referring to is when she thought I was suspicious and tried to murder me. Twice.

I didn't do anything on either occasion. All I did was stand there basically peeing myself in fear as blades snapped over my head.

Actually, both of those broken swords are still hidden in the bushes over there.

"But this time it's different. My will is focused and honed to levels hitherto unseen. I won't fail like that again."

S-sure. It's nice that you're so pumped up, but do you have to swing the sword around?

Come on, Zenobia, you know I'm not a bad guy. You've said so yourself, right? So there's no reason to cut me down, right?!

"I've learned from my past two defeats! Today, victory shall be mine!"

"Ar-arwf?! *(H-has nothing changed?!)*"

This isn't a game! You know I'm not a monster, so there's no need to kill me!

"Don't be afraid! I'm not going to kill you! Just some fur! I'll just cut some fur!"

That doesn't make me feel any better! It's clear as day you want to test your sword out on me!

"Here I goooooooo!!"

"Arwwwwwwwf!! *(Noooooooooooo!!)*"

Zenobia closes the gap in an instant, her sword slicing through the air.

The blade glints right in front of my face, giving me no time to even think about dodging before it gets split right down the middle.

The sword, that is.

"*Unnyaaaaaaaa?!*"

Zenobia lets out a strange cry.

The blade made a nice, crisp sound as it snapped; the *cling* almost sounded like a musical instrument. I guess it really was high quality.

The broken end of the sword twirls through the air before vanishing into a nearby bush.

"M-my sword... Th-three years' pay..."

"Arwf... *(Yeesh, I thought I was a goner... No matter how many times you do that, I'll never get used to it...)*"

Just like the previous two times, I'm completely unscathed. No damage at all.

I guess I was aware of this already, but my body's crazy tough, huh?

The first time this happened, I just assumed Zenobia's sword was a fake, since it wasn't able to cut me or even hurt me, really.

And no matter how fluffy my fur is, there's gotta be something else that's preventing the pain.

Maybe this Fenrir body of mine simply has really high defense.

Huh? But when Len bites me it really hurts...

"Arwf... *(Wow, mouse teeth are incredible...)*"

"Squeak... *(Call me a dragon... 'A dragon's fangs are incredible' is more like it...)*"

Len mumbles a sleepy rebuttal from her napping spot in my fur.

"Arwf, arwf. *(Right, right, my bad, my bad.)*"

Oh well, RIP to Zenobia's three years of wages.

"Ahhh... Sword... My sword..."

Zenobia stares at the sky, flabbergasted.

A perfect representation of grief. Normally I'd say she got what she deserved, but this sight is too pathetic.

"Arwf. *(I hope you learned your lesson. Quit it with the dangerous antics already.)*"

I paw at Zenobia, who is still gripping the hilt of her broken sword.

"Wh-what are you doing...?"

"Arwf, arwf. *(There, there.)*"

Zenobia is befuddled by the head pats. No matter how good my little paw pads feel, she's had enough of it.

"Tch, what a disgrace...!"

And to the victor go the spoils. In this case, a trembling Zenobia with a bright-red face.

Hee-hee-hee, there's my favorite sight. I wanna lick her.

Zenobia's angry face is just too cute; I should paw at her some more.

Paw paw paw paw. Ah, *paw paw paw paw paw paw.*

"E-enough already! Y-you're taking it too far!"

Whoops, she's escaped.

"You may have won today, but I won't lose next time!!"

Are we seriously going to do this again?

Looks like she'll keep trying until she's bankrupt.

And then we'll have broken swords pouring out of the bushes.

"I'm not going to lose agaiiiin!!"

"Arwf, arwf. *(Yeah, yeah.)*"

And with these parting words, Zenobia runs off and I return to my nap under the tree.

† † †

"Thus the hero Routa and his seven companions went off to the spirit world to defeat the terrible Demon Lord."

"Arwf. *(So with the hero, it was an eight-man party? They probably only took four into battle and left the rest back with the wagons. I bet they left behind members like a wizened old mage and an elderly knight.)*"

I'm listening to my lady read her book aloud.

The hero gathers his companions, topples the five generals of the Demon Lord's army one by one, and then triumphs over the Demon Lord in a final showdown.

It's an easy-to-read hero story for kids.

It sounds like the kind of story that would typically appeal to boys, but Lady Mary really likes it, so I end up hearing her read it a lot.

"Arrrf! *(I've already heard this story a million times, but getting to hear my lady's cute voice makes it all worth it. I'll listen to you read as much as you like!)*"

As she goes along, Lady Mary brushes my neck with her slender fingers.

Hee-hee, being petted feels so good. Keep it up.

"Squeak... *(Grr, you've got that slovenly look about you yet again...)*"

Len's irritated face pops out.

Hey, just because you're on good terms with Lady Mary doesn't mean you should poke your nose out whenever you want. My lady is kindhearted and gets along with anyone, but what'll you do if someone else sees you? You're a mouse, the sworn enemy of chefs and maids.

Not to mention that things would be a hundred times worse if you turned into a dragon.

"Squee-squeak... *(What exactly is it about this child that entrances you so...? When I assume a human form, you always claim I'm too young for you... Your perversions are absolutely incorrigible, darling...)*"

That's rude. I'm not a pervert—I'm completely normal. And I definitely don't want to hear it from a spinster dragon with a puppy fetish.

"Oh, little mouse. Good morning."

"Squee! *(Hmph!)*"

Len shoots a venomous glare at Lady Mary, but she doesn't notice and simply smiles back.

"Would you like me to pet you, too, little mouse?"

My lady's fingers find their new target, and she begins delicately scratching Len's tiny head.

"S-squee... *(Ah, no, stop that! Stop that, I say! Fwaaaahhhhh...?!)*"

"You like it here? Or maybe over here?"

What amazing technique. A single touch from those skilled fingers caused Len to melt.

"Squeeeee...! *(I said shtaaaapppp... Shtaaaapppp... Afwahhhh hhhh...)*"

I get the feeling that the strongest person in this household isn't Len, or I, but Lady Mary.

† † †

"Arwf, arwf... *(Time for food, glorious food! I wonder what's for dinner today...)*"

"Well, look who we have here. You're right on time, Routa."

Old man James seems to be on his break after the lunch rush. He looks over at me.

Heh-heh-heh, I know I can usually score something freshly made if I show up right as Lady Mary and the rest of the family are about to have a meal.

It's too hard to wait when you can smell all the delicious scents wafting from the kitchen. I'm already at my limit!

"Woof! Woof?! *(Hey, old man! What's on the menu tonight?!)*"

"Just hold your horses. If I don't do this in order it'll all fall apart."

With that the old man takes a large set of tongs and pulls a few choice morsels from the stew pot.

He piles slow-cooked meat along with rough-chopped chunks of vegetables onto a plate.

He then pours a rich broth over the top to complete the meal.

"There you go, pot-au-feu. An easy enough dish to make that hides a lot of subtleties."

Hey, I recognize this. I've never made it myself, but I have eaten pot-au-feu before at diners.

"Arwf, arwf! *(Time to dig in!)*"

Y-yuuum! It's completely different from anything I ate in my previous world.

The individual ingredients are all still structurally sound. The potatoes are nice and soft, and the carrots are so tender they practically melt in my mouth.

The sausages add a level of saltiness that's pleasantly subtle when mixed with the broth.

And finally, the pièce de résistance: the heaping chunks meat. The moment I put a piece in my mouth, it begins to melt away, then explodes with flavor.

"I marinated boar ribs overnight in salt and wine vinegar. You love it, don't you? Another way to get the meat that tender would be to use carbonated water, which keeps the meat juicy, but it's hard to get your hands on any. If only it weren't so difficult to transport..."

Eating is my specialty, regardless of preparation methods. But the old man seems to enjoy talking about them. Like Zenobia and her endless knowledge about weaponry. I'm just gonna tune it all out.

While the old man is distracted with talking, I take the opportunity to slip Len some of the food.

"Squee, squee, squeak... (*My, my, this is delectable. I thought freshly hunted meat was without peer, but this is far superior. This 'cooking' practice is most intriguing. It certainly does wonders for the flavor...*)"

Len sits there nodding and harrumphing as she chews. She's even listening to the old man's stories with a lot more attention than I am.

It's good that you're interested, but please try not to blow your cover.

Chefs and mice have a history of conflict.

"Miss Miranda, we just found this jammed under the door in the entranceway..."

"Oh, what is it?"

Right outside the kitchen come the voices of Miranda and Toa, two maids of the household.

The maid with the large breasts and glasses is Miranda, whereas the short one with small breasts is Toa.

"It doesn't say who it's from nor who it's for."

"Indeed, and the mailman didn't come today. Whoever brought it to the mansion must have slipped through the gate and across the courtyard. But no one saw anything."

The mansion is out in the countryside and surrounded by forests. Even by carriage, it takes a few hours to get to the nearest village.

Surely there's no one who would come all the way out to such a remote place only to play a prank.

"I wonder if we should give it to the master?"

"Well, it seems to be a simple envelope. How dangerous could it be? We'll give it to him after the meal."

Hmm, a letter from an unknown sender… Definitely intriguing. I think I'll tag along.

"Arwf! Arwf! *(But before that, I need to polish off this delicious food!)*"

I gorge on pot-au-feu until the stew pot is completely empty.

† † †

"Hrmm, a letter. And with no addressee written, nor anything else. Well then, let's open it and have a look."

After we've eaten, Papa relaxes in the living room and takes the letter from Miranda.

He picks up a letter opener and sticks it into the envelope.

"PLEASE WAIT!!"

The sudden cry stops Papa in his tracks. I'm just as shocked as he is.

There stands Zenobia, one hand outstretched to halt Papa.

"Wh-what is it, Zenobia?"

"Master, do not let your guard down. You shouldn't carelessly open something when we have no idea who sent it. There might be poison or some magic curse within. We just don't know."

"Wh-what? I—I can't imagine that would be the case……"

Well, Papa is filthy rich and a noble of some repute, so Zenobia might actually be onto something.

"I will open it and inspect it. Is that acceptable?"

"I suppose I can't simply dismiss your worries. If you would, then, Zenobia."

"Yes, sir."

Zenobia takes the letter from Papa and then casually tosses it aside.

Wait, what is she doing?

As the thought crosses my mind, she pulls a new sword from the sheath around her waist.

There's a sudden flash. An instant later the envelope is cut into shreds. The naked letter flutters to the ground, and Zenobia's hand goes still.

"Hmph, looks like there's no danger..."

After carefully checking the letter and confirming that it's safe, she passes it to Papa.

"As splendid with the blade as ever. I couldn't even follow your movements."

Weird. Zenobia just did something that made her seem like a real knight.

But she's not really Zenobia without the trademark helplessness. Maybe she has a fever? I'm worried.

Papa seems to be in a good mood after witnessing the skills of the freeloader knight.

But as he opens the folded letter, his face stiffens.

"Wh-what's this...?!"

"What's wrong, Father?"

Lady Mary rushes up to Papa and glances at the letter over his shoulder as he reads aloud.

"'This is a warning. You are a corrupt lord who consorts with demons. We shall be visiting tonight to relieve you of your mansion's riches. Signed...The Silver Wing Bandits'?"

I don't really get it, but everyone else in the room freezes.

Did he just say "warning"? What the hell? Like those calling cards that master thieves like Lupin send before committing their crimes?

"An advance warning! Wow! Just like in the stories!"

"M-my lady, this isn't the time to be excited. They said they would come *tonight*..."

Miranda's face is pale as she lays a hand on Lady Mary's shoulder, still trembling with excitement.

"The Silver Wing Bandits...? This is the first I've heard of this organization. And they're quite brazen to send warning before the heist. Or perhaps they have a different motive..."

Papa leans back in the leather sofa, absorbed in thought.

The man runs a huge company and holds the noble rank of marquis. Of course he's not going to be unnerved by some unexpected notice of an impending crime. He's too cool.

"The letter mentioned my riches, but... They didn't write exactly what they were after, so I haven't the foggiest idea what the target could be."

Fair. They could take any single piece of furniture and make a fortune.

In fact, depending on your definition of *riches*, you could include most things in the mansion.

"But of all my riches, the most precious to me is my Mary."

Papa throws in a dashing wink, but my lady has devoted her full attention to wondering what kind of burglars the Silver Wing Bandits might be. There's no getting through to her.

"M-Mary..."

Poor Papa.

But the second-most important treasure has to be me, right?! Say it's me!

"Are you here to comfort me? Thank you, Routa."

I cuddle up to Papa, and he pats me on the head. I'm satisfied.

"Anyway, what are we going to do about this? There's too much left shrouded in mystery. If only we knew what they were after, we could simply give it to them and put this all behind us."

Papa does prefer to avoid unnecessary conflict.

But he's being naive.

If we give them one thing, they'll want to take another, and then a third, and then a fourth. That's how people think.

If you keep giving in to their demands and handing things over, next thing you know, the pantry is bare and there's nothing left to eat.

...Hold on a minute, when did this become about me?

"Master, please leave it to me! I'm here to deal with problems like this!"

Zenobia crows and puffs out her chest.

"You've shown me such kindness by allowing me to stay here. Please allow me the opportunity to return the favor!"

"Oh, thank you, Zenobia." Papa's face brightens. "I was actually just thinking I had no choice but to ask for your assistance. I don't have the time to contact the guild or hire guards by this evening. I'm sorry to call upon you like this, but please help us."

"Of course! And these villains, these scoundrels, who would dare accuse my master of corrupt and heinous crimes—I'll wet my sword with their blood!"

"Hmm, while I'm grateful that you think so much of me and the family, I am hoping for a more *peaceful* solution. Something that avoids killing."

Papa tries to keep Zenobia's zeal in check.

"Then I'll use the blunt side of the blade!"

"Ah, yes, the blunt side should be... Wait, isn't that sword double-edged...?"

It wouldn't make a difference. With Zenobia's gorilla strength, anything could become a lethal weapon in her hands.

I wonder if Gorillanobia could even hold back if she wanted to.

"Right then, I'm off to start my rounds! Everyone make sure to lock up all the doors and windows, and I ask that nobody leave their room tonight!"

Wow, Zenobia's a lot more fired up than she usually is.

Usually she moves even less than I do. And I'm the family pet! Oh well.

She's a hardworking freeloader of a knight. I guess she's trying to shed her deadbeat stigma.

I'll cheer her on from my bed.

"Arwf, arwf. *(Now then, my lady. Thieves are scary, so let's hurry up and go to bed. I'll be your teddy bear.)*"

I push Lady Mary out of the room with my head.

And then someone grabs me by the scruff of the neck.

"Where do you think you're going? You're coming with me."

"Arwf?! *(Huh?! Why?!)*"

"You're the family guard dog! It's time for you to get to work!"

"Arwf, arwf! *(I work all the time! I provide emotional support as the family's beloved pet!)*"

"Stop resisting…!"

"Rrrggh…! *(I! Don't! Wannaaaa…!)*"

Zenobia's yanking on my collar, and I'm resisting with everything I've got.

Give it up, Zenobia! You're pulling all my scruff to the front and making me look silly!

"*Pfft… hnk…*"

Look over there! Toa looks like she's about to die laughing! Think of the children!

Isn't there anyone, anyone at all, who will help me?

Ah, Lady Mary. Lady Mary is watching.

I'll have to beg for help.

"Arwf! Arwf! *(My lady! Save me, my lady! Your adorable pet is being abused!)*"

"Zenobia! You can't just take Routa! I want to join you on the night watch as well!"

Wait, *that's* what she's worried about?!

Trust our little tomboy to worry about missing out on the action.

"C-certainly not, my lady. Come now, let's get ready for bed. Toa, please double-check the doors and windows and inform the rest of the staff."

"Y-yes, ma'am."

Miranda leaves the living room with Lady Mary in tow.

"I'll be heading to my room as well. It doesn't look like I'll be getting any work done tonight."

Oh no, even Papa left.

Which leaves one victorious Zenobia and one incredulous Routa.

"…Are you still going to resist?"

"Arwf… *(I'll come quietly…)*"

† † †

"I'll patrol the second floor. You patrol the first. We'll meet each lap at the staircase of the great hall."

"Arwf… *(Fiiiine…)*"

I wave my tail in response to Zenobia as she springs up the stairs and begin my patrol of the manor.

"Arwf, arwf. *(I know we all kind of got caught up in the moment, but aren't people normally afraid of bands of thieves?)*"

What do I do if I find the thieves and they attack me? It'd be a huge loss if anything happened to the family pet.

"Squee. *(There isn't a thing in the world that would be able to harm you, my darling.)*"

Idiot. Even if I'm 100 percent safe, scary things are still scary. Super-scary. That's just the kind of dog I am.

"Squeak. *(Your vigilance makes you all the more desirable, my beloved… Oh my, did I say 'desirable'? That's so embarrassing~)*"

Even if you blush, I can't find you cute. You're still just a dragon masquerading as a mouse.

Your human form was a little endearing, but that's only because you looked like a kid. Either way, you're outside of my strike zone.

"Arwf, arwf. *(So my body really is super tough?)*"

Being able to fire laser beams and break swords with my face isn't very useful for pet life, but those abilities do come in handy in times like this.

Guess I better give thanks to that ditzy goddess.

But wait. If I weren't a monster to begin with, I probably never would have had as many problems!

Tch, now I'm just contradicting myself.

"Squeak. *(You're Fenrir, King of the Fen Wolves. What nonsense are you spouting? How could any beast who defeated me, the great Lenowyrm, be weak? Even in your youth, you are still the most ferocious of all. Yes, you will truly make a fitting groom, my beloved.)*"

With emphasis, *no thank you.*

I'm fed delicious food, and I sleep and play whenever I like. I'm more than happy just cruising through life like this. So I'm sorry, but I'll have to decline your proposal.

And if any villains—such as these thieves—try to get in the way of my happy pet life, I'll use this Fenrir body to turn the tables on them.

I stand up on my back legs to try out some shadowboxing, but I'm still in a canine body, so it comes off as more of a silly waddle.

Also, I'm still rather afraid of fighting. Maybe if I find the thieves, I can just run away and get Zenobia. Yeah, that sounds like a plan.

With that decided, I continue creeping quietly down the hall.

"Arwf, arwf? *(Even the maids have retired early. It sure is quiet, isn't it?)*"

All the others have locked their doors and are shut up in their rooms, as Zenobia requested. This prevents amateurs from clumsily roaming about and then being caught and used as hostages by the thieves.

It's Zenobia's fault that I'm thinking like this.

I'm a bit uneasy that we only have two guards, but, well, if Zenobia's reputation as a former top-rank adventurer isn't just for show, I'm sure she'll be able to handle things.

…She'll be able to handle things, right? If there was ever a time that she absolutely had to be at the top of her game, this would be it.

"Mrooow. *(Routaaa. I've come for a late-night snack. Gimme gimme.)*"

Following the voice, a hole opens in midair and a cat falls out of it.

Damn it, Nahura's back yet again. While she looks like nothing more than a strangely colored cat, she's actually the familiar of a powerful witch.

But instead of using her magic for noble causes, she uses it to come over and steal food whenever she's hungry. What a waste of teleportation magic.

"Arwf, arwf. *(Pretty brazen from someone who isn't even a house cat.)*"

"Squee. *(Exactly right. And riding about on my darling's back without permission, no less. Brazen indeed.)*"

I don't think someone who's living in someone else's fur has the right to say that.

"Mrow? *(Oh, come on, you're going to get mad* now, *after all this time?)*"

Nahura puts her forepaws up to her face and acts all bashful. Now, that's cute.

And so, with one animal on my head and another on my back, I continue off down the hallway.

"Mew? *(Awfully quiet tonight, isn't it?)*"

"Woof, woof. *(Oh, right. Apparently, some burglars are gonna show up tonight.)*"

"Mrow?! *(Burglars?! …Hmm? How do you know they're on their way?)*"

"Squeak. *(They sent advance warning.)*"

"Mew? *(An advance warning? Why would burglars do that? For what purpose?)*"

"Arwf? *(I have no idea. Why* would *they do that?)*"

Papa was also curious about that part. One possibility is that it was simply to scare everyone in the mansion.

Or maybe someone just wants to play pretend as a phantom thief?

"Bark. *(Maybe they're trying to distract us with one thing while they go after something else.)*"

If you think about it, that's always one possible outcome of a warning.

If you're told what the target is, you'll do whatever you can to protect it. Look at us. We've got only two people on patrol, and we're both guarding the inside of the mansion, leaving absolutely no one to watch the outside.

Which must mean that the thieves aren't after some treasure inside the mansion, but rather something nearby.

"M-mew?! *(D-did Routa just say something intelligent?!)*"

"S-squeak?! *(Are you all right, darling?! You didn't eat something strange, did you?)*"

"Arwf—? *(Okay, you know what—?)*"

Just as I am about to retort, my stomach growls.

"…Arwf. *(…Maybe we should eat first.)*"

""MrowSqueak! *(Agreed!)*""

That's about the level you can expect from us three stooges.

I turn toward the kitchen and off we trot.

"Mrow? *(What shall we have today? We just had ham recently. Are there any new smoked meats?)*"

"Arwf, arwf… *(Well, I'm pretty sure that back when I was eating the pot-au-feu the old man said something about making spare-rib bacon…)*"

"Meow! *(Bacon sounds great! I love bacon!)*"

"Arwf. *(There's no way it'll be ready to eat yet.)*"

First you have to brine the meat, then slow-smoke it. It's a pretty lengthy process.

I'm always stealing some, so I've become well acquainted with how it's made.

It almost seems like he's started smoking more meat for me than for everyone else in the mansion.

Sorry for the trouble, old man. But thanks as always.

And with my heart full of newfound appreciation, I'm off to steal more food tonight. *Drool.*

"Arwf…? *(Huh? Do you hear voices coming from the kitchen…?)*"

I hear female voices whispering to each other.

Maybe some of the maids got hungry. Everyone was shuffled off to bed early today, so who knows, maybe someone missed dinner?

You shouldn't break the rules, little maids. You'll have to be punished.

And by that I mean I'm going to surprise you and make you split your snack with me.

"Arwf… *(All right, you two, pipe down…)*"

"Squee… *(You're going to do something foolhardy again, aren't you…?)*"

"Mew… *(Ooooh, I love playing pranks…)*"

I crouch down and creep toward the kitchen. I lift my forepaws up to a window.

I slowly raise just my head and take a peek inside, and there I see…

† † †

"Got it. We're in," says a girl to her two companions while returning her lock-picking tools to her pouch.

"Keep quiet. The lights aren't on, but they've probably posted guards."

The tallest of the girls adjusts her hair ornament.

"Well, that's why we wrote the warning letter. It draws the attention of the guards away and gives us the chance to sneak in," responds the shortest as she pushes up her glasses.

The two of them follow after the girl who picked the lock, and they sneak into the room.

While there are differences in looks and physique, the three girls all share common features.

Like the silver hair and the long ears. Not to mention the inhuman beauty. All signs of the long-lived elves.

The elves trespassing in the mansion all seem very serious as they tiptoe around in light clothing.

"Where should we start our search?"

"I wish we knew more about the layout of this mansion. I didn't have the time to investigate."

"And what about our sisters? Who knows what they will be forced to endure while we take our time investigating? The sooner we can make this evil lord cough up wherever he could be holding them, the better."

"Eruru, please don't suggest such horrid things…"

"I'm with Ururu. We're not actually a gang of thieves. We're just here to save our sisters."

"I'm sorry, Oruru. It's just that we've been living as bandits for so long. I mean, just look how good we've gotten at breaking and entering…"

"Come on, you call us bandits, but all we've been doing is stealing food in the dead of night. And no one knows who we are, so we'll be fine. We'll just keep doing this until we save our sisters, and then we can find a nice, peaceful forest, gather our scattered friends, and rebuild our village."

"Right. We've been searching for so long, and we've finally found a clue as to their whereabouts. We must succeed!"

"Yes, we've got reliable info that the slavers who abducted our sisters are connected to Faulks Co. by way of Morgan Trading. There's a good chance our sisters have been sold."

"I've heard the lord of this manor takes in girls with debts or no place to go and then employs them as his maids. He probably makes them do all sorts of unseemly things."

"Tch, what a disgusting abuse of power…!"

These elves sure seem riled up over hearsay.

"Anyway, what kind of room is this? It's shockingly clean…"

"Well, judging by all the tools, I'd say it's a kitchen."

"Dang it. How do we always manage to break in to the food storage part of the house…?"

"W-well, whatever. As long as we make it inside, we don't need to sweat the details."

"Whoa, look at this flour. Typical rich people—they've always got the best ingredients."

"Wow, you're right. You could bake some quality bread with this stuff…"

"Don't get distracted, you two. Let's keep going."

At her urging, the other two reluctantly walk away from the bag of flour.

"First, I'm going to check on the hallway. When I give the signal, follow me."

As the one called Oruru checks the hallway, she notices that something new has captured the attention of the other two.

They stand there, mouths agape, staring up at the window.

"Oh, for—I told you two to get it together."

"Oruru, Oruru…!"

"Ah! Ah! Ahhh…!"

What has them so spooked? She follows their gaze until she sees *it*.

Looking down on the three elves are six glittering eyes.

"Wh-what the…?!"

Its size far surpasses that of the girls, and it gives off an intensely intimidating aura.

Why would a monster be here? Does the owner just let monsters have the run of the house?

These sorts of thoughts race through the minds of the girls, but they're too scared to speak.

They're elves. They grew up in the forest, they've come face-to-face with demons, and they're more than skilled at determining an opponent's strength. But even going back through everything they've faced, they've never encountered anything like this.

Their sixth sense is screaming at them.

Here's where we get eaten and die, they think.

"Ee—eeeek……"

The beast's giant, jagged, drooling maw opens wide, and—

""""WoofMrowSqueak!"""""

The creature lets out a strange cry, causing the three elves' faces to contort in silent screams before they faint on the spot.

† † †

"Arwf...? *(Huh? Did we just manage to subdue the bandits without lifting a paw?)*"

We peeked through the window after hearing the voices, but the three girls fainted without us having to do anything.

I leave the window and head into the kitchen.

"Arwf, arwf. *(These three girls don't really seem cut out to be bandits.)*"

They're not quite what I'd imagined.

Because they went as far as sending an advance warning, I was expecting someone more like a cool middle-aged master thief kind of person.

And while they are definitely wearing lightweight clothes reminiscent of thief gear, these three are young ladies.

Judging by their long ears and silver hair, is it possible they are elves?

They remind me of a certain witch. And given that she and they have the same distinctive facial features, it's highly possible they're of the same race.

"Squeak. *(Careful, darling, you're drooling.)*"

"Arwf. *(Oh, my bad.)*"

I started drooling because of the delicious smells wafting out of the kitchen. It wasn't because I saw these girls and thought they looked tasty. Of course not.

"Mrow. *(So what should we do? We can't just leave them here.)*"

"Arwf, arwf. *(We're out of options. Guess we'll have to get Zenobia.)*"

And speak of the devil—Zenobia is standing right there at the door.

"You were late to the meeting point, so I came to check on you, and w-were you about to eat them...?!"

"Bark, bark?! *(You're way off! How do you see this and jump to that conclusion?! These girls just fainted!)*"

"I'm kidding. No doubt they saw you and were so surprised they fainted, right?"

Thank God she understood. My heart can't handle that kind of joke.

And excuse me? Why would anyone faint after seeing a cute pet like me? How rude. *Harrumph.*

"Anyone worth their salt is going to take one look at you and know exactly how much of a monster you are. Hmm, are they elves? I suppose you couldn't have done anything against their acute senses. But still, I've never heard of elf bandits before."

I knew something was off. Elves don't really strike me as the bandit type.

"We'll have to inform the master, and he'll decide what to do with them. I'll restrain them, so you go and fetch him."

"Arwf, arwf. *(All right, all right.)*"

It doesn't really feel like snack time anymore, but maybe he'll give me a treat.

I head up to the second floor and softly bark outside Papa's room.

"Arwf, arwf. Arwf, arwf. *(Papa, get up. We caught the burglars.)*"

"What is it, Routa? You haven't caught those thieves already, have you?"

Papa slips a gown over his pajamas and peeks out the door.

"Arwf, arwf. *(I did indeed. Well, we say 'caught,' but they kind of just fainted all on their own.)*"

"I don't see Zenobia with you—is she watching over the thieves? And did she send you to get me?"

"Arwf, arwf. *(As sharp as always.)*"

"Well then, I'm on my way. But I'll need you to guide me, Routa."

"Arwf, arwf. *(Just leave it to me.)*"

I lead him downstairs to the great hall, where Zenobia has the three elf burglars tied up together.

"These girls look young enough to still be called children. Are you sure they're the ones who sent the letter?"

They're elves, so they probably don't look their age, but they also really don't look like they'd be in some dangerous line of work like robbery.

"U-ughh……"

The taller elf is coming to.

Her unfocused eyes pass over the room before suddenly locking on Papa.

"Y-you! Are you Lord Faulks?!"

"Ah, exactly right. And you would be the thieves who sent the letter, I presume?"

"Tch, you're more corrupt than I'd imagined, keeping a beast like that in your mansion..."

"Beast? Do you mean Routa here? Our family dog...?"

Papa glances over at where I'm sitting next to him.

"Well, I suppose he has been getting a bit large lately. Have you been eating a little too much, Routa?"

H-have I? Maybe it's your imagination? I guess I should probably go on a diet.

"I don't think his food intake is the problem..."

Zenobia groans before brandishing her sword and pointing it at the girl.

"Eek...?!"

"It's fine to be confident, but don't go thinking you'll get away with breaking in to our house and attempting to rob us."

Whoa, scary.

After being targeted by the sudden bloodlust, the other two girls begin to stir.

"Ahhh, awawahh..."

"Shoot, we've been caught..."

Unlike the other two, who are coming to terms with the situation, the taller girl the sword is pointing at continues to glare at Papa.

"Damn you, Faulks, you corrupt noble! Return my sisters!"

What sisters? And "corrupt noble" couldn't be further from the truth.

"Well now, I fear there may be some sort of misunderstanding. Why don't you tell me a little bit about why you're here?"

Typical Papa. Even when facing thieves who tried to rob him, he's calmly assessing the situation.

"......Very well."

She tells us the whole story of how she and the others came to find themselves in this situation.

They were living in a peaceful village in the woods when they were suddenly attacked by a gang of humans.

Out on the frontier, beyond the oversight of the kingdom, such slave raids occur, though infrequently.

Most of the elves were able to abandon the village and escape, but there were still several who were unable to flee and were captured.

Their gang of three was originally a group of five, but their two eldest sisters, who saved them and helped them escape, were captured in their stead.

In fleeing from the humans, the villagers were scattered, and the three girls pooled their skills to survive.

Now they pretend to be bandits and live day by day, stealing from scoundrels and continuing to search for their captured sisters.

"*Uuunh*, you've had it so hard...!"

Zenobia is bawling in sympathy.

I don't get to see you cry that often, Zenobia. I wanna lick you.

"And so you heard a rumor that your sisters are here."

Based on the information that their sisters had been sold to the Faulks family, they had come here to rescue them.

According to the rumors, Papa used his money to gather the finest girls as his slaves and indulged in a sumptuous feast every night.

When they heard in the Royal Capital that the Faulkses had had contact with the slavers, they thought for sure that their sisters had been bought and pursued them to the mansion.

"Arwf... *(Papa...)*"

"Hmm. So that's the sort of rumor that's been spreading, is it...?" Papa's shoulders slump dejectedly.

"It's utter nonsense."

Miranda consoles Papa as she appears, carrying a lantern.

She's wearing a cape over her night wear and cuts a much different figure from when she's wearing her normal maid outfit.

"Certainly there are those among us from less-than-pleasant backgrounds, but we were all saved by Master Faulks. We are all thankful toward him, and not one of us bears a grudge. We work here in the mansion as maids of our own free will. We are all officially hired through the company and receive proper wages. Whatever you've been imagining is completely false."

"Wh-what are you...?!"

Oh, thank goodness. It's all bogus.

For just a moment there, I was envious—ahem—*suspicious* of Papa.

"So you're saying that our sisters aren't here after all...?!"

"Aw, man, but it took so long to get here..."

"Where could they be...?"

The three of them start crying, and we don't know what to do.

"It is true that I was introduced to slavers during our stay in the Royal Capital. But I'm strongly opposed to slavery. I don't even think we should allow debt servitude or penal servitude anymore. I did think it strange that I was introduced to such people, but perhaps it was simply to sully my reputation..."

"D-did you see any elves?!"

"No, I left the meeting location as soon as possible and couldn't tell you who was in there. I'm sorry..."

"I see..."

The girls look so dejected, and I can't think of anything to say to them.

"Well, at least the misunderstanding has been cleared up. Zenobia, untie these ladies."

"Are you sure?"

Zenobia sniffles as she responds.

The girls in question look dubious about being released.

"Y-you're letting us go…?"

"Well, I'm fairly confident that you're not going to take anything now. And seeing as there haven't been any crimes reported in the area, I can't think of any reason—as the marquis—to arrest you, either. After listening to your story, I'll also use my company's resources to aid in the search for your relatives. Hunting people is a violation of this country's constitution. It might take some time, but it will no doubt be better than searching haphazardly."

"Why would you go so far as to help us…? You know nothing about us, and we're just burglars, of a different race, no less…"

"If I abandoned someone in need, I'd never be able to look my daughter in the eye. I want my daughter to be proud of her father. That's all that matters to me."

He's the embodiment of compassion and human kindness. Man, what a guy. Papa, you're the coolest.

"And if you're having troubles and you'd like, I could see about getting you some work through my company."

"Thank you…but we'll continue searching for our sisters on our own. Could you tell us about that group of slavers? I think we'll restart our search there."

"We just want to help them as soon as possible, you know?"

"Yeah, what they said."

The three girls seem pretty set in their decision.

"Arwf… *(I wish there was more we could do…)*"

There didn't seem to be anything I, a pet, could do to help, but I still didn't feel right sending them off like this.

"I really did only meet with the slaver for a brief moment. The only thing I can say about the man is that it was impressive how *little* of an impression he left... I'm sorry I can't be of more assistance. At the very least, please allow me to cover your travel expenses. Miranda."

"Yes, Master Faulks. I assumed you would offer, so I brought this."

Miranda walks back into the room carrying a leather pouch on a silver tray.

"Y-you really don't need to go that far!"

"Please, accept it. Otherwise, I'll worry about what might befall you on your journey. And I can't have you stealing anything in my domain, now, can I?"

Papa laughs that last bit off as a joke, but it's really not a laughing matter.

"Thank you. We'll definitely repay this kindness."

The tallest elf girl accepts the leather pouch before apparently being hit with a thought.

"Oh, right, this is a tool the people who attacked our village used. Maybe it's a clue that can help us track down our sisters?"

From her pack she pulls out a collar adorned with a round stone.

"Arwf? *(Huh? Haven't I seen some of those before?)*"

But where was it?

"Squeak... *(Wasn't it in the capital with that showy girl? You know, the noisy, uppity one...)*"

Ah yes, that Goldilocks with the twin drills, Lady Elizabeth.

Len was right; the monsters Drillizabeth had each wore one of those around its neck. And they all were imbued with brainwashing magic.

When she was showing off her collection of *pets*, the spell snapped, and they all went berserk.

After that, Drills befriended Lady Mary and became a considerably dedicated pen pal, but I'm almost positive this is the same collar.

"Hmm. No, I don't recognize that. But it might be useful as a lead. Do you mind if I borrow it?"

"Not at all—please do... I always thought of humans as nothing more than vicious creatures, but you've shown me that there are kind ones as well. I apologize for the late introduction. My name is Oruru."

"I'm Eruru. Thank you for everything."

"And I'm Ururu! Thank you!"

The three girls decline Papa's offer to stay the rest of the night and depart in the morning, and instead they say their good-byes and leave the mansion.

I break off from Papa and the others, who are sadly watching them go, and slip out the back door into the night.

"Woof, woof! *(Hey! Wait up! Hey~!)*"

My barks surprise the three sisters.

"Wh-what is it?! Are you going to eat us after all?!"

"W-we don't taste good! H-how about you eat these grilled dumplings instead?!"

"A m-monster wouldn't want something like that! W-we've gotta run for it...!"

They're terrified. Time to use my ultra-cute pose to show I'm not a threat.

"Ha-ha-ha. *(See? I'm not scary. But I wouldn't mind those dumplings.)*"

I'm splayed on my back and wriggling back and forth.

"Y-you didn't come here to attack us...?"

"Arwf, arwf. *(Look how fluffy I am. I'm not a mean monster! Just a cute little doggy. And I've seen those collars before, so I thought I'd come tell you what I know.)*"

Weird. I'm showing them my cutest puppy tricks, but all three of them still look like they want to run away.

I guess they can't understand what I'm saying. That's going to make communication difficult.

"I can't believe such a strong monster would willingly be subservient to humans."

"That's true, but they did say it was a dog…"

"Whatever this so-called pet is, I think it has something important to tell us. So do you know something about those collars?"

Huh? So they *do* understand what I'm trying to say?

"Oh yeah! What do you know?!"

"Arwf?! *(Can you guys understand me?!)*"

The taller elf, Oruru, draws closer to me.

It must be because she can understand what I'm saying. Maybe elves can hear me?

"We can't understand your barks, but we've made a connection through your magic," the middle elf, Ururu, replies nonchalantly.

"There's probably a lot of people who can understand you among the powerful races with strong magical sensitivity, like us."

I stare at Eruru, the short elf with the glasses, with a "What the hell did just you say?!" expression.

That could have been bad. Thank goodness I didn't have any weird thoughts about licking the three of them.

Speaking of which, Hecate's always just talked to me normally. I thought it was just some special ability, but maybe it's a racial thing.

Wait, have I always been transmitting my thoughts like that? There's just too much I don't know about this body.

Damn that airheaded goddess who sent me here without explaining everything.

"Well? Where did you see those collars?"

"Arwf, arwf. *(I saw them at an acquaintance's house. I don't really know that much about it, but I bet she'd tell me if I asked her.)*"

Only question is how to ask.

Drills doesn't understand me, and even if I asked Len to transform and interpret, who would trust a little girl upon first meeting her? These three would have the same problem.

"Mrow? *(Oh well, then why don't we ask my mistress for help?)*"

Ask Hecate? She's certainly more reliable than the rest of this motley crew...

She's always bailing us out of trouble. Should we really be begging for her help this often?

"Mrow. *(Routa, Routa. My mistress and I share our senses.)*"

"Arwf? *(And?)*"

"Meow. *(Mistress is always eagerly awaiting chances to leave her workshop, so it should be fine to call on her whenever—gack!)*"

"That's enough of that...!"

A heeled shoe stomps down on Nahura.

A panicked witch appears from midair and lands before us.

"A-arwf? *(H-hey there, Hecate. I guess you could hear us, huh?)*"

"Routa, would you please forget everything Nahura just told you?"

"Arwf, arwf... *(Oh, uh, I wasn't really paying attention...)*"

"So you didn't hear anything. *Right?*"

"A-arwf. *(Um, of course.)*"

Crap, she's intense. And with the way she's not letting her words trail off, I can tell she's serious. She's scary enough that I wouldn't wanna mess with her.

"Mew, mew— *(My mistress may act above it all, but she can actually be quite lonely and is always happy when people ask her for assistance—gerk!)*"

Nahura never could recognize danger. RIP.

"Wh-where did she come from...?!"

"Sh-she just came out of the sky, right...?!"

"Ummm, who is this?"

The three sisters are bewildered by the sudden appearance of the witch.

"Oh, my apologies. I'm Hecate Luluarus. Pleasure to meet you."

The sisters jump as Hecate grabs her skirt and hat and sweeps into a theatrical bow.

"L-Lady Luluarus?!"

"From the legends...?!"

What's this? Is Hecate some elf celebrity?

"Elves normally live to be about three hundred years old, but Lady Hecate has lived for over one thousand years! She's the legendary elder!"

"She was an elder even before our grandmother was born!"

"Lady Luluarus is the eternal elder!"

The girls are super-excited, but all they're doing is incurring Hecate's wrath.

"…Perhaps I should leave?"

"A-arwf, arwf! *(Wait! Wait! Please don't go!)*"

Time to shut up about her age, girls. Otherwise Granny Hecate is going to storm off in a huff!

"I—I apologize."

"I'm sorry."

"I'm sorry, too."

The three girls apologize.

"So what brings you here, Lady Luluarus……?"

"Arwf, arwf. *(Hecate lives in the forest near here. And she's also the family doctor.)*"

"I also figured I should help my fellow elves."

Hecate should be able to tell them about Drills and give them some info about the collar. She seems to be an important person in the capital, what with founding the Adventurers Guild and such.

"Bark, bark! *(Okay then, Hecate, I'll leave it to you!)*"

Take care, have a nice trip.

If she shares senses with Nahura, she should know all about what happened at Drills's place.

My work here is done. Time to head home and hop in bed with Lady Mary.

"Stop right there."

Huh? I should be walking, but I'm not moving forward. Why are my legs just treading air?

"I've never met the girl face-to-face. Wouldn't it be easier if someone she knows is with us, Routa?"

It would indeed.

I float back to Hecate's side like a cat being held by the scruff of its neck.

Damn. Levitation magic sure is useful.

"Well then, we'd best be off. You wanted to save them as soon as possible, right? Tonight would be ideal."

"That's impossible. Tonight, you say? Even by carriage, it takes a month to travel to the Royal Capital…"

With Papa's airship we managed to do it overnight. I guess that's how long a carriage takes, huh?

But still, don't worry. This amazing witch can use her magic to get us anywhere in an instant.

"Wait for me!" Zenobia cries out as she appears from the mansion.

I guess she overheard our conversation somehow.

"Lady Hecate, please allow me to accompany you."

"Oh my, whatever for?"

"For protection! I've already received permission from Master Faulks."

"Oh my, for protection? Don't you think I'll be fine with Routa here? Not to mention my own abilities. I can't think of a reason that it would be incredibly necessary."

"But I…"

Zenobia flashes a glance toward the elf girls.

She sobbed when listening to their story. Maybe her feelings toward them have changed.

Unable to convince Hecate to let her come along, Zenobia just stands there fidgeting.

Hecate gives her a stern look before her expression suddenly softens.

"I'm kidding. I'd be glad to have you join us, Zenobia."

"Oh! Th-thank you so much!"

Maybe the initial refusal was only for show, to test Zenobia's intentions.

That whole "protection" bit is nothing but a front. Clearly she wants to come along to help out the three sisters. But she also can't come right out and say she wants to help the people who just tried to rob the Faulks family, who have been hosting her.

I think Hecate wanted to make Zenobia a little more self-aware.

"Arwf. *(She's unfortunately not blessed with good sense.)*"

Zenobia does stuff like this a lot, which is probably why Hecate tried to be mean and scare her.

But come on, Hecate, I know you. Even when you seem to be picking on someone, you're still looking out for them. You're just trying to act cool, aren't you?

"Is there something you'd like to say?"

"Ar-arwf. *(N-nope, nothing at all.)*"

Something terrifying lurks in her narrowed eyes. Don't look at me with that kind of smirk. You're going to make me wet myself.

"Then, as I said already: We'd best be off."

Hecate lightly taps the ground with her staff, and a shining white circle begins to spread.

It surprises the three girls, who try to jump out of the way, but only a moment later we're standing in the middle of a city.

"Wha?! Wh-where are we…?!"

"This is the Royal Capital."

"Th-the Royal Capital?!"

"We traveled all the way here in an instant?! No way! Was that the teleportation magic that was lost during the war with the Demon Lord?! I can't believe it! I can't believe I actually saw it!"

The elves stand there with their eyes wide and jaws dropped. A nearby drunk drops his bottle of booze.

Is this type of magic really that special? We use it all the time.

"I chose this place because there aren't many people, but it means we'll have a slight walk."

"Which way are we headed? It's still the middle of the night, so it'll probably be hard to search for our older sisters."

"Let's not get ahead of ourselves. How about we start with some food?"

"""*Food?*"""

Oh, right, I haven't had my midnight snack yet.

But it is pretty late. Are there still going to be shops open?

Hecate seems to have a place in mind and takes off.

"Please wait, Lady Hecate! These streets can be dangerous at night! I'll lead the way!"

As Zenobia moves to take the lead, Hecate grabs her by the shoulder.

"I'll be fine. Take the rear guard, if you would, Zenobia."

"Of course, b-but..."

"I. Will. Be. Fine. Okay?"

Her tone will brook no arguments. Clearly Hecate knows a thing or two about Zenobia.

This knight would lead us with the utmost confidence but would almost definitely lead us in the wrong direction. And we can't let someone with such a horrible sense of direction lead us. Zenobia goes silent and drops to the rear.

In the end, we've got me walking alongside Hecate, then the three still-nervous sisters, and finally Zenobia, muttering to herself as we head into the dark city.

"Arwf, arwf? *(Hey, Hecate. Is it really okay to just not investigate those collars?)*"

When she was saying we'd sort things out tonight, I thought for sure we'd have to invade Drills's house to question potential suspects about the collars.

"It's fine. They'll come to us."

Come to us? How does she know something like that?

Sometimes I don't understand what Hecate's doing. Well, she still hasn't led me astray, but at times like this I've still got questions.

"Woof, woof? *(By the way, what district is this? It's definitely not as clean as where we were last time we visited the city.)*"

"We're in midtown, somewhat close to downtown. I wouldn't say it's dangerous, but it's also not a place I recommend walking around by yourself."

Was it really all right to bring the girls here, then?

"But you're here with us, Routa. You'll protect us, right? We're counting on you."

"Arwf, arwf. *(Ha-ha-ha, that's enough of that.)*"

No, seriously, please don't count on me. I'm just a house dog, not a guard dog.

Zenobia's more suited to violence, so if some punks try to make trouble, it's up to her. A pet like me is just going to turn tail and hide.

We continue walking down a street lit solely by streetlamps for a few minutes.

"Arwf, arwf. *(Something smells good.)*"

With every step we take, the street is getting brighter, and more and more people can be seen walking about.

Steam carrying the scent of food wafts through the night air, mixing with the sounds of revelry and swishing alcohol.

"Are these all bars?"

"A lot of them are. This area is quite popular at night."

Based on the seductive ladies waving down the male pedestrians, some of these shops are of the more seedy variety.

But the witch standing next to me is definitely a class above them when it comes to being sexy.

"Whoa, look at that beauty!"

"And what about that monster next to her?! It's wearing a collar! Is that her familiar...?!"

"A mage, a swordswoman, and three rogues? That's an unusual group for an adventurers' party. Looks like they're going to Bordolf's place. Hope they don't come in here."

It's no surprise that our little group is beginning to draw attention, and it seems people are whispering about us.

"This is the place. Shall we go in?"

Hecate stops in front of one of the bars.

"Arwf, arwf? *(Are you sure they'll let me in?)*"

I'm an animal, after all, and usually shopkeepers kick us animals out for hygienic reasons.

Though with my daily baths, I'm probably cleaner than most of the guys around here.

"It'll be fine. I know the owner."

And with that, Hecate pushes through the swinging doors and into the bar.

"Arwf, arwf? *(What should we do?)*"

"Squeak. *(If Lady Witch says it will be fine, then it will be fine.)*"

"Mrow. *(More importantly, I'm starving.)*"

Now that she mentions it, I am, too. Thanks to those three elf girls huddled behind us, I missed my midnight snack.

And the delicious smell of grilled meat emanating from the pub has made my mouth start watering again.

Right, I'm going in. And if I surprise or scare anyone, I'll deal with it then—by stealing meat from one of the tables and making a break for it!

"Arwf... *(Howdy...)*"

It certainly seems like a popular place. A number of round tables are scattered throughout the large room, and everyone seems to be drinking and having a great time.

There's also a fair number of staff. Waitresses are scurrying among the customers, delivering food and drinks. Everyone's smiling. It looks like a nice pub.

"Arwf. *(Now, where'd Hecate......? Ah, there she is.)*"

Hecate struck up a conversation with the muscled middle-aged bartender as we were fussing about outside.

He must be the owner of this place. He has white combed-back hair and an eye patch, kind of like a pirate. And with his muscles and stern expression, this hulking middle-aged guy looks completely different from old man James back home.

"I never thought I'd see you again during my lifetime."

"While it's always fun to talk about your apprentice bartending days, I'm here on other business today. Mind if I take some seats upstairs?"

"Enough of that. Don't go bringing up the embarrassments of my youth. We've got a reservation for up there tonight, but if you're fine with sitting near them, go ahead."

"Thank you. How about I come by with Emerada next time and the three of us share a drink?"

"...Give me a break. You're just going to drink the place dry... Who's that? Is that group by the door with you?"

The white-haired bartender looks past Hecate and over to me just as I enter.

"Yes, they're friends of mine. Very dear friends."

"You're always dragging around some strange folk... So long as it doesn't have any diseases or fleas... What is it? A wolf? A monster? Something like that?"

"Woof, woof. *(I'm a dog, thank you very much.)*"

Just look at how nicely groomed I am. And I have a master, and a lady, and maids.

"...Well, if it's with you, then I don't have any complaints. You go along and wait upstairs and I'll bring something up for you."

And with that dismissal, the eye-patched bartender heads back into the kitchen to relay the food order.

As instructed, we head up the stairs to the loft seating on the second floor.

The first floor is packed, but up here it's almost like we're alone. Kind of feels like a VIP seating area. *Bwa-ha-ha*, look at us. So much better than the drunks.

Hecate is draped over one of the chairs at a table. I sit next to her, and then the three sisters perch tensely on their chairs. Zenobia does a quick sweep around the room before finally sitting on Hecate's right.

"Arwf, arwf? *(Hey, Zenobia, what's with that look? Were you really that put out by not being able to lead us?)*"

"Keep it down. Don't raise your voice in here...!"

Zenobia is slumped in her seat, as though trying to avoid being seen from the first floor.

Maybe there's someone here she doesn't want to meet. Based on all the weapons, there seem to be a lot of adventurer types here.

Actually, she did something similar last time we came to the Royal Capital, hiding behind me when we were outside the guild headquarters... Seems like there might be a troubled past there.

"Wh-why are you looking at me like that...? I'm not hiding from anyone. I left the Adventurers Guild in good standing."

And yet you're still trying that hard to hide.

I narrow my eyes as Zenobia turns away.

Hecate watches the exchange with amusement.

And while this is going on, the food arrives.

"Arwf, arwf! *(Woohoo! This looks delicious!)*"

It isn't the fancy cuisine of the manor, but instead an overflowing assortment of hearty, high-calorie dishes.

Little fried shrimp still popping from the fryer.

Garlic toast topped with salted pork fat.

A juicy, leafy salad decorated with crispy fried bacon.

Juicy, tender skewers of what seems to be teriyaki chicken.

The look, the sound, the smell—everything here is to die for.

I'm overcome by appetite, and a great tummy rumble rings out.

"Arwf?! *(Wait, huh, that wasn't me?!)*"

"""".................""""

The three elves try to hide their blushing faces.

"Well then, why don't we all dig in? Those who believe in the gods can say their own prayers."

Seems like Hecate isn't the praying type, since she's already serving herself some of the bacon salad.

"Arwf! Arwf! *(Me too! Me too!)*"

"Of course—here you go."

"Arwf! *(Thanks!)*"

I dig into the salad that Hecate hands me.

The texture of the leafy greens and crunchy bacon is unbelievable. The salt of the bacon and the dressing is absorbed by the greens and doubles their flavor.

"Arwf, arwf!! *(So goooood!!)*"

It's a walk in the park to make simple bar food, so why does it taste so good?

"And it goes great with beer."

Hey now, we're here to save the elves' sisters. Do you think this is the right time for drinking? How disgraceful. I'll have some, too.

"Ruff!! *(This beer is so light and refreshing!!)*"

I don't know if it's unfiltered or just cloudy, but it's smooth and washes away the lingering oil in my mouth. This must be why Hecate recommended the place. What a great bar.

""""*Gulp…*""""

Watching us eat must have pushed the three girls to the limit, because they quickly clasp their hands and rattle off a prayer before falling on the food like savage beasts.

Looks like they haven't been getting enough to eat. They're shoveling it down like they've missed a few meals.

"Slow down. You'll choke."

Zenobia, who had been the first to start praying and the last to finish, offers Ururu some water as she pounds her chest and groans.

Zenobia may be a meathead, but she's got impeccable manners. She eats in the same polished manner as Lady Mary: using a fork and knife and taking small bites.

"It's been a while, but the flavor hasn't changed. It's certainly delicious."

After eating the toast with the dribbling pork fat, Hecate licks the crumbs off her fingers in a display of poor table manners. It may be rude, but it's also sexy as hell.

"Mewf! *(This chicken is delicious! The sauce is sweet and spicy, and the flesh is so tender!)*"

"Squeak, squeak! *(And this shrimp! It's so crispy!)*"

Nahura and Len seem satisfied. But make sure you don't drop any on my back, okay? Once it gets into my fur it's a nightmare to get out.

"It's delicious—so delicious."

"How long has it been since we've had a proper meal?"

"I wonder if our sisters are getting enough food?"

The three girls are still gulping down the food, with Zenobia stepping in to help if they start choking.

"Slow down and chew. No one's going to take it from you. You want to save your sisters, don't you? Well then, first you have to be healthy."

Zenobia warns the three of them while rubbing their backs.

Oh, look at Zenobia acting all motherly. What a gentle gorilla.

If she ever finds out I call her Gorillanobia, she'll do whatever it takes to end me, so let's keep that our little secret.

"E-excuse me!" splutters the shortest elf with the glasses—errrr, Eruru, was it? And her voice sounds like she's moments from bolting.

"Why are you being so nice to us?! You only met us today, and we tried to rob you!"

"Arwf? *(Tch. Do we need a reason to help someone?)*"

"Mew. *(When you talk with your mouth full of food like that, we can't understand anything that you're saying.)*"

"Squee? *(Besides, darling, didn't you try to leave this to someone else so that you could head home?)*"

So mean. I was just trying to look cool.

The three girls pretend I didn't say anything and stare at Zenobia.

"Just like the marquis before: You're not simply forgiving us but even going as far as to help us to search for our sisters."

"There's really no reason for you to do all this for us, and it's got us on edge!"

These elves, whose village was attacked and sisters were kidnapped, have never experienced kindness from humans. So it seems the gentle demeanor of the people at the manor has them especially uneasy.

Zenobia looks straight at them and answers their doubts.

"I, too, was saved by the Faulks family."

Zenobia has said she was an adventurer before going full freeloader.

"When I became disillusioned with the adventurer life and was lost and adrift, they did not hesitate to take me in. I had lost faith and trust in everyone, and they rescued me."

When we first met and she treated me as an enemy, she was just trying to protect those in the mansion. I know how much Zenobia cares about everyone.

"And in turn, my lord would say that he has been rescued. People are all connected to one another. Whether helping or being helped, those in the Faulks family are all connected in some way."

I see. The reason the mansion is so warm and inviting is that everyone there cares for one another. It feels so natural living there that I didn't realize it.

"What I'm doing is simply an imitation of what the people of the Faulks family did for me. So please don't feel any obligation toward me. I'm doing this because I wish to. And that's my only reason for helping you."

Zenobia's still being so cool today...!

She's gotta have a fever or something, right? I'm really getting worried.

Without the gorilla grunts and chest pounding, she's just not Zenobia.

"M-miss..."

"Wow..."

"You're so cool!"

The three girls stare at Zenobia with flushed cheeks.

Hold up, now. I basically said the same thing, so what's with this huge difference in reception?

"Probably in the delivery, I'd say."

Urgh. Hecate delivers the finishing blow.

"So anyway, yeah. Keep eating. After that, we'll be off to save your sisters. Lady Hecate is a peerless sage, and I'm sure you remember my abilities... And that wannabe dog has his uses as well."

Oh, Zenobia seems a little embarrassed.

But what she said contained one little mistake. She made me out to be a stand-up guy, when I'd be happier lying down.

Don't make the therapy dog do any real work!

† † †

We've finished our meal and are relaxing with some tea when Hecate looks toward the stairs.

"Well then, it should be about time..."

Immediately after Hecate murmurs, I hear faint footsteps coming up the stairs.

Must be another customer. Upon reaching the second floor, they head quickly to their table without giving us a glance.

This must be the customer with the reservation the owner mentioned earlier.

This loft seating must be reservation only, because aside from us, this is the only customer.

"............"

Their hood is pulled low over their face, but they seem rather short and quite slender.

Maybe a woman? No, but this isn't the sort of place for a woman to come to alone this late at night.

"Hmph... It appears they have yet to arrive. And yet they were the ones to invite me. Clearly they don't have the proper courtesy a merchant should possess."

Taking a seat, they lower their hood.

Amazing curls of blond hair spill out.

"Arwf?! *(Wait, Drills?!)*"

What is the loudmouthed, monster-loving Lady Drillizabeth doing here?

"Right on time."

Right on time? How did Hecate know Drills was gonna be here?

I look at her with a doubtful expression, but Hecate just sits there swirling her wineglass and smiling.

"Squeak. *(Hmph, Lady Witch certainly is mysterious.)*"

"Mew. *(My mistress's attitude is just for appearances. She puts on an act, but inside she's not actually planning anything evil—ngah!)*"

I wonder if Nahura's been stricken with an illness that makes her say stupid things that might get her killed.

"Mewl! *(Mistress, forgive me! Forgive me!)*"

I say a quick prayer for Nahura, who's under the table getting stepped on.

"Excuse me, you there, please quiet down. I'm here for an important meeting..."

Drills, who has turned to scold our group, suddenly freezes.

"A-are you—are you that lovely dog I met before?"

"Arwf, arwf. *(Indeed. I am that lovely dog.)*"

Only Drills would say such a thing. And I like it. I still won't be your pet, though. But I hope you maintain that obliviousness.

"Wh-what are you doing here? Is Mary with you?"

She's definitely not here. Though she probably would've been thrilled to come along.

We're planning to save the sisters of these elves behind me, and I couldn't bring myself to lead her into danger.

But on that note, what's Drills doing alone in a place like this? I wouldn't exactly call this area "safe."

If she'd brought her dragon, Christina, as a bodyguard, I think that would've been suitable protection, but it doesn't seem Christina is with her today.

But then again, if she had brought Christina, it would've caused a huge commotion at the bar. Even if she paid off the guards to keep them quiet, there's no way she would've been able to quell the uproar of the townsfolk.

"You're Mary's family doctor, correct? And you're the knight I remember seeing when we saw Mary off. But you three are unfamiliar to me…"

She approaches our table without hesitation—every bit the daughter of a skilled merchant—and strikes up a conversation.

"Why are you here? It doesn't seem like you're on another vacation."

"Indeed. I'd like to explain, but I think you have something to discuss with them first?"

We turn to look in the direction Hecate is pointing just as a few men begin climbing the stairs.

"Ah! We'll speak later. I must speak with these gentlemen first."

Drills adopts a serious expression and returns to her seat.

Hecate gives a slight gesture with her outstretched finger just as Drills turns to walk away.

She appears to write a few characters in the air, and while I can't understand what it might mean, it surprises Drills.

"Arwf, arwf? *(What did you just do, Hecate?)*"

"Hee-hee, you'll see."

Hecate is especially sexy when she's being coy.

While this is going on, the men reach the top of the stairs.

At the forefront is a small man wearing a silk hat and a gentleman's suit. He slaps on a greasy grin and heads over to where Drills is sitting.

"Oh dear, I'm so sorry to keep you waiting. And it looks like you came alone, as promised."

Hmm? *Alone?* We're sitting right here.

"Squee. *(It's invisibility magic. Just as the blond child sat down, Lady Witch erased our table's presence.)*"

I guess that gesture with her finger just now was for a magic spell.

Drills probably looked surprised because we suddenly disappeared, but she sure caught on quickly.

Tch, clearly Drills has a better head on her shoulders than I do. And here I thought we were birds of a feather.

Five burly guys stand behind the man in the silk hat. They're all wearing matching long-sleeved coats. They must be burning up.

They don't take a seat, but instead assume a protective formation, standing in a half circle around the table. Looks like these guys can't see us, either.

"What are they going to do to her...?!"

"Shh, wait. Just watch."

Zenobia must realize there's a spell between us and them, as she silences the sisters and observes Drills.

"You seem to be better off than the last time we met."

"Well, of course, that's because of your patronage, my lady."

Wow. The way he's rubbing his hands together is super sketchy. Mix that with his smirking face, and his sliminess just doubled.

I don't think I'd ever buy anything from him. He doesn't seem cut out to be a salesman.

"Well then, should we order some drinks? And perhaps some food to go along with them? This may be a dingy bar, but the food here isn't half-bad."

"I'm fine, thanks. Why don't we just get down to brass tacks?"

The merchant slaps his palm in an exaggerated manner in response to Drills's curt refusal.

"Then let's get to it. For you, my lady, this time we've successfully procured a large number of rare animals. We thought that before we sold them to the market as pets, we would let you have the pick of the litter, so to speak."

By "rare animals" he means monsters, I'm sure.

Of the animals Drills used to keep in her house, every one is a monster. Now they all live in the forest protected by the Fen Wolves, but none of them should've been kept as pets in the first place.

I guess Drills never quite learned her lesson and still sees those monsters as regular animals.

Barring exceptions like Christina, I imagine it's difficult for monsters to form attachments with people. And relying on those enchanted collars is just going to result in another stampede when the spell wears off.

Drills's parents aren't very close to her, and the neglect fed into her loneliness. She started buying all those "pets" to fill the void.

But I kinda thought we resolved that issue last time.

Now she's got Lady Mary as a friend, and I was almost certain her bond with Christina had changed after all the other monsters ran away.

But it looks like even my lady and Christina aren't enough to heal Drills's loneliness.

And if that's the case, that's pretty tragic.

"If you'd like, I could take you to see them right after we finish here?"

"No, there's no need."

Drills's response doesn't match my expectation.

She shuts down this discussion about pets and tosses a leather sack on the table in front of the merchant.

"This is double the amount of our prior arrangement. I'd like you to take all the animals back to where you found them and release them."

"Release them…? What caused you to change your mind?"

The merchant isn't looking at the sack of money but instead at Drills with an inquisitive expression.

"I've come to realize that my actions were a mistake. I realized that I shouldn't run from my loneliness, but rather confront my issues with my father and mother directly."

Even though she shouldn't be able to see us, Drills shoots a glance in my direction.

"Some very dear friends taught me that. And there's no solace to be found in keeping animals locked away in cages."

My little Drillizabeth is all grown up. There's no trace of the girl who did whatever she pleased, laughing and not caring about the trouble she caused those around her.

"Oh? And I don't suppose that in addition to confronting

Mommy and Daddy dearest, you'll be bringing up our little arrangement?"

The merchant sneers at Drills's attempt to end their business relationship.

"Surely you've picked up on the fact that I'm not the most honest of merchants. And don't you think that if it became public knowledge that Daddy's little girl had done business with such a shady character, it might negatively impact Daddy's company?"

"...Are you threatening me?"

I've got a bad feeling about this. Drills is trying to put on a brave face, but I can tell she's becoming overwhelmed.

"No, no, of course that wasn't a threat. I completely understand what you're thinking, and I think you've made a wise decision... By the way, what happened to those pets you bought before?"

"Well, they......they all ran away."

"Oh, they ran away, did they? I'd think if something like that happened, it'd be the talk of the town. But I haven't heard anything like that."

Yeah, that's because Nahura teleported all of them to the forest. I guess from Drills's point of view it must have looked like they vanished in an instant.

"Are you accusing me of lying?"

"Hmm, that you *don't* appear to be lying has me all the more confused."

The merchant strokes his chin and frowns.

"Well, to be honest, I didn't expect you to still be alive after being attacked by the monsters."

"What?"

If we hadn't been there back then, those monsters would've been all over Drills. Even with Christina jumping in to protect her, they probably still would have killed her.

But that's not the problem here. Based on what he just said, he knew the collars were faulty from the get-go. Maybe they were designed to fail from the start.

"Our expectation was that the monsters would be driven mad and kill everyone in the house, but thanks to some sort of miracle, everyone seems to be fine."

Bull's-eye. I was right.

"I thought it would be the perfect opportunity to undermine the Morgan Trading Company. But instead they've started dealing with that damned Faulks Co., which is the last thing we want."

"Wh-what are—what on earth are you saying?!"

"Now I've got to clean up this whole mess. The original plan was to lead you to some remote location and kill you, but based on how things are going, you probably wouldn't come quietly, would you?"

The merchant puts his silk hat back on as he steps back, and the bodyguards move to block Drills from escaping.

"It may be a bit conspicuous, but we'll just have to do you in right here."

At that signal, one of the men begins to move his arm. From the sleeves of his coat he draws a long, curved knife.

He swings the sharp, glittering blade down with the intent to slash Drills's face.

"Arwf. *(Yeah, I've seen enough.)*"

I put myself right in the path of the knife. It strikes my back and then snaps pathetically.

I've been hit by Zenobia's best strikes over and over. Some amateur attack like this isn't scary at all.

"……Arwf. *(……No, wait, that was a lie. I definitely peed a little.)*"

Even if I know it's not going to hurt, scary things are still scary! Acknowledge the courage it took to make that leap!

"What the—?! Where did this monster come from?!"

"I don't remember selling something like this?!"

And I don't remember being sold by someone like you. I was sold by a legitimate pet shop, which makes me a pedigreed pet!

The man whose blade broke stands there looking like he can't believe what just happened. From his perspective, it probably looks like I appeared out of nowhere. But the truth is, I've been right under their noses the whole time.

"K-kill them both!" the merchant shrieks. But not a single one of the men responds to the order.

"Nice job stopping him, Routa."

As Zenobia speaks, the bodyguards slump to the floor.

While my jumping to Drills's defense drew their attention, Zenobia took care of them. We make quite the team, don't we?

All Zenobia had to do was whisper, "Sic 'em," and I leaped into action. That's terrifying. What if I'd messed up? Stop putting your confidence in me, please.

"Now, my lord did ask me to avoid killing anyone. Which is the only reason I used the flat of my blade on scum like you."

The flat of her blade? I'm pretty sure she just smacked them with her bare hands. I guess that as a knight, she thinks of everything in sword terms. Looks like our family's problem child is more meathead than gorilla.

"Trash like you isn't even worthy of my blade. Do yourselves a favor and stay down. I wouldn't want to sully my sword with your filthy weakling blood."

But you're fine with trying out new swords on me, huh? I don't think "people you're willing to cut" is a group I need to be in.

"Tch, what a useless bunch of...!"

The merchant tries to slink off, only to find his path blocked by the three sisters.

"Don't try to run away!"

"You're going to tell us where our sisters are."

"Shall we torture him?"

He knew about the collars, so there's no doubt he's involved.

Torture or not, these guys did just attempt to murder someone, so we'll have to hand them over to the guards. Although I'm sure there's a lot we can talk about before that happens.

"You, youuuu...!"

Whoops, forgot about Drills. Looks like she fell into shock after almost being killed.

Here's a special freebie. My fur is perfect for calming down.

It's just a matter of time before the merchant is taken into custody. Zenobia's guarding the front, and the three girls have the rear. And the bodyguards are all unconscious, so he doesn't have any support. And we've got plenty of witnesses to the crime.

Everything is under control.

That said, it doesn't seem like the merchant is ready to give up yet. He keeps scowling at us.

"Hey, you guys! What the hell are you doing in my bar?! If you're going to fight, do it somewhere else! Outside!"

The owner heard the disturbance and stomps up the stairs.

We're somewhat busy at the moment, so please don't come up.

"Tch!"

Just as I hear the merchant click his tongue, the sound of the window shattering rings out. He took the moment's chance and leaped through it.

"Arwf?! *(Did he just jump?!)*"

Suicide by jumping is never a good idea, because you might fall on someone below you. I did a fair bit of research on the subject back when I was stuck working for my dead-end company, so I'm rather well-informed.

Wait, this isn't the time to be thinking about depressing crap like that.

I rush to the window and look below.

"Arwf! *(Whoa, no way!)*"

The merchant jumped from the window, kicked off the wall of the neighboring building to get to the roof, and is now escaping across the rooftops.

Those aren't the movements of a short, fat guy.

"Arwf? *(What is he, some kind of ninja?)*"

"With those moves, he's obviously not an ordinary merchant…! But even with that leg strength he won't be able to escape me!"

Zenobia climbs up onto the window frame and leaps into the night.

With one bound, she's on the roof of the next building and off after her merchant prey.

"Bark?! *(Huh, wait, should I go, too?!)*"

I'm worried about letting Zenobia go off on her own. She really has zero sense of direction.

"Hold on, there, Routa."

As my forepaws are on the windowsill and I'm puzzling about whether to go or not, Hecate calls out to stop me.

"Arwf? *(Shouldn't I go after them?)*"

"They'll be fine. Let's let him escape rather than catch him."

Hecate seems to have an idea. She was gracefully sipping her wine throughout the entire ruckus.

"Damn it, I told you there was going to be trouble." The owner shows up with a sour expression.

"You didn't say anything about that."

"Didn't I? Oh well, I'll be adding the cost of replacing the window to your tab."

Hecate pouts, and the owner gives a bitter laugh as he begins to clean up. He doesn't seem very interested in what just occurred.

"Oh, don't touch the glass, ladies. I'll take care of it."

Rather than worrying about the glass, shouldn't we be worrying about what to do with these unconscious guys? Shouldn't we tie them up or something?

I guess it was Zenobia's crazy strength that knocked them out, so they probably won't be waking anytime soon.

And is this some kind of everyday occurrence? The people on the first floor don't seem worried at all.

They went quiet for a moment, but then the noise immediately picked back up.

"Will you add their charges to my tab, please?"

Drills has regained her composure and addresses the owner.

After he acknowledges her with a shrug, she moves over and takes a seat facing Hecate.

"Allow me to introduce myself. I am Elizabeth Morgan. I am most grateful to you for saving my life. I would like to thank you."

In a complete reversal from her prior stuck-up behavior, Drills gives a deep bow.

"And I would appreciate it if you could explain some of what just happened. I seem to be somewhat involved."

"Well if you're offering to treat me, how can I refuse? Why don't we walk and talk? Thank you for everything, Bordolf."

"Sure thing. I've already contacted the guild, so we're fine here. And it looks like the payment is covered."

"Arwf! *(Thanks for treating us, Drills!)*"

Free food is the best food.

The owner waves to Hecate as she heads down the stairs, and we follow.

After settling the bill, we proceed outside to find the night has darkened even more, and it's gotten a bit chilly.

"Arwf, arwf? *(So Christina really didn't come along?)*"

I guess the crazy girl who rode a dragon everywhere she went really has disappeared.

"Hey, human." The tallest elf, Oruru, calls out to Drills.

"What is it?"

"Didn't you hear him asking about Christina?"

"Who's Christina? A friend of yours?"

She's a land dragon with horrible taste. And by the way, I didn't ask you to interpret for me.

"Christina is watching the house. She never really liked walks anyway, and I've stopped showing her off to the townsfolk."

Looks like Drills has seen the error of her ways and is even ashamed of her past actions.

"Wait!! Can you—?!"

Drills suddenly sidles up to the elf girls.

"Can you three understand what animals are saying?!"

"No, we can't understand animals, but this guy isn't an animal. He's actually a high-ranking monster, so—"

"Woof! Woof! *(Shut up, elf girl! Shush!)*"

What do I do if Drills blabs to Lady Mary and she finds out I'm not a dog?! My sweet setup as a pampered pooch would be ruined!

"That's amazing! Do you think there's some way that I could learn to understand them?!"

"Um, well, wh-who knows? Maybe people who aren't elves just can't understand them…"

"Is that so…? That's a pity. I just thought it would be fun to be able to talk with Christina…"

Trust me, you don't want to do that. That chick likes it when you step on her, Drills, and she'd tell you about it in great detail.

"Arwf…? *(Man, are all dragons perverts?)*"

"Squeak. *(You are the last person I want to hear that from, beloved.)*"

"Mew. *(You should probably look at yourself first, Routa. Maybe start with your species.)*"

"Woof. *(I'm a dog. Just a cute, lovable, fluffy pet dog. With cute little button eyes.)*"

"S-squee! *(They're blind. Those eyes of yours are blind!)*"

"Meow? *(You try your absolute best to deceive even yourself, don't you?)*"

As we rehash familiar arguments, we continue to follow after Hecate.

"So I asked before, but what brings you all back to the Royal Capital? Mary and Mr. Gandolf aren't with you, so I assume they aren't involved with this matter?

"That would be correct."

Hecate gives a quick rundown of the situation.

The elf girls are searching for their sisters, who were kidnapped to be sold as slaves.

And the soldiers who caught their sisters were using the same collars that Goldilocks once had on her pets.

And because of that coincidence, we came to the Royal Capital to ask Goldilocks about what she knows.

But before they could ask her, they discovered the merchant, the root of this evil, who no doubt knows the whereabouts of the elves' sisters.

Goldilocks interjects with a few questions during the story but seems to get the gist of the situation.

"So then, isn't it all the more important that we catch the merchant?"

"Before he ran off, I attached an anchor to him, so we can find him at any time."

"Oh, an anchor…?"

It seems Hecate and Nahura require these anchors to target their jumps when using their teleportation magic.

They've also got one attached to me. Stealing my privacy. And my food.

"But I suppose it's about time."

Hecate waves her staff.

A shining white portal opens, and Zenobia appears.

"Bastard! You think you can escape from me?!"

Zenobia is grinding her teeth, head flicking back and forth.

That's definitely the look of someone who got lost.

She loses sight of someone, and instantly she gets lost. Just one of those Zenobia qualities.

"What? Lady Hecate?! When did you—?!"

Looks like she didn't even realize she'd been recalled. Just as you'd expect from a woman who's all brawn and no brain. She never wavers.

Also, it looks like you can recall the target, not just warp to it. This teleportation magic sure is useful.

"And so what will you do, Elizabeth? If you'd like to head home, perhaps we could escort you?"

"No, I'll be joining you. I may not have known what the collars were, but I still purchased them, and I feel some responsibility."

What a gallant response. The Morgan Trading Company is in good hands. Now if only they could do something about that pet food that's only good for nutrition. When food tastes bad, it ruins everything else.

"Very well, now that we've joined forces, shall we head off to our final destination?"

And again Hecate activates her teleportation magic, allowing us to remain in hot pursuit of the merchant.

† † †

"*Haah-haah...* Did I get away...?"

That chick was crazy fast. I'm a top-class spy and she still almost caught up to me.

If I hadn't gotten lucky with them losing sight of me, I wouldn't have been able to make it back to the hideout.

The silk hat was lost long ago, and the suit is now a mess. His hair sticks to his forehead with perspiration.

He no longer has the appearance of a rich merchant but instead looks like any other poor little man. Even the expression on his face is so generic that no one would think him the same merchant if they met him anywhere else.

"Guess that job's a bust..."

The place he barely escaped to is a warehouse not far from the city's harbor.

"Who'd have thought she'd have allies like *that*...? And to think I dismissed her as a harmless little girl..."

The assassination was a failure. The plan was to harm Marquis Faulks, who is close to the imperial family, by damaging the reputation of the Morgan Trading Company, which Faulks Co. recently took under its umbrella. But after this debacle, it won't be easy to make another move on the marquis for a while.

Looks like there's no option but to get out of town and lie low while waiting for the next opportunity.

He opens the door to the warehouse and slips inside.

The dim warehouse is filled with cages housing monsters caught all over the country.

Each of the monsters is wearing a collar and cowering with lifeless eyes.

"Well, that was only one of many plans to overthrow the royal family, and there's no reason to leave any evidence behind. I can release the monsters to rampage through the city while I escape on a ship in the confusion."

The mission may have been a total failure, but if he can cause at least a little injury, it won't have been a complete loss.

And releasing the monsters into the city is bound to cause considerable damage.

It doesn't matter if they don't cause any damage at the city's center, since most residents live on the outskirts beyond the downtown.

If an incident were to occur in the supposedly impenetrable Royal Capital, then trust in the royal family would waver.

Once they've been commanded by the collars to go on a rampage, the monsters should break out of their cages and terrorize the city. Good enough for a last-ditch effort.

"But before that... I have some property I need to collect."

Slipping through the gaps, he makes his way deep into the collection of cages.

He pulls a cloth from over one of them, revealing two women lying inside.

"You two are rare commodities. You'll be useful down the road."

What beautiful silver-haired elves. He captured them when he raided the elf village on the edge of the kingdom. Two perfect specimens.

He could sell them for getaway money, or they could be used as catalysts for forbidden rituals or magical weaponry. Plenty of ways they can be used to assist in overthrowing the royal family. It would be such a waste to leave them here.

A few of these elves were among the group that protected the noble's daughter he tried to assassinate. If those elves are related, they may have heard something about these two.

So rather than just dumping the elves here, he'll have to take them with him.

"Get up."

"…Urgh."

In response to the man's order, the two elves begin moving and slowly rise to their feet.

"Please……let……us……go……"

Although clearly exhausted, the elves glare at him with determined eyes.

"You really are a race with strong intellect. The magic has very little effect on you… Looks like we'll have to increase the power of the spell."

The orders don't render them unconscious, but the elves' bodies still respond to them, and they walk out of the unlocked cage.

"Hurry up. Once we get out of here, I'm releasing the monsters."

"We will never……forgive you……"

"Shut up and come with me."

The elves' throats forcefully constrict, and they follow the man toward the exit.

The door is thrown wide open with a roar.

† † †

"That's far enough, villain!"

The moment we materialize, Zenobia hears the voice of the merchant and plunges into the warehouse.

Typical meathead. Doesn't wait for the right moment, doesn't make a plan—just barges in without thinking.

"Arwf! *(Wait, this isn't the time for thinking. He just said he was going to make the monsters riot. We've got to stop him!)*"

"Squeak. *(Even were they to rampage, you could defeat them. It would be easy for you, darling.)*"

Damn it. I'm surrounded by meatheads. I am a pet; I'd prefer a peaceful solution.

We chase after Zenobia.

"Tch, what are you doing here......?! I thought I lost you—were you just waiting to see where I went......?! Who the hell are you bastards?!"

"I don't normally tell villains my name, but for you I'll make an exception!"

Zenobia slides her sword from its scabbard and points it at the merchant.

"I am Zenobia Lionheart! And I am the one who will destroy you!"

"What?! Th-the Zenobia Lionheart?!"

"The SS-Rank adventurer! Slayer of One Thousand Men! Fortress Destroyer! Labyrinth Annihilator! The Blood-Soaked Knight with the Heart of a Lion! The Crimson Lionheart!"

A pile of stupid nicknames come pouring out of the merchant's mouth. Dang, if Zenobia wouldn't be the coolest thing to a teenage nerd.

"So Zenobia Lionheart herself has gotten involved...... That must mean the guild knows what we're up to...... I was supposed to be the trapper, but instead I find myself caught in the trap......!"

The merchant glares bitterly at Goldilocks.

"Oh-ho-ho-ho! What a simpleminded fool!"

Look, I get you're feeling happy we've won, Goldilocks, but you had no idea what was going on.

"You're a fine actress. To have fooled someone like me for so long......"

All Zenobia did was give her name, and he seems to be working himself into a panic.

People with those stupid nicknames are amazing.

"Damn it, I guess it's come to this......?!"

The merchant pulls out a hidden dagger, drags one of the elves in front of him, and holds it to her throat.

"Stay there! If you come any closer, I'll slit her throat!"

"Oh my, what a naughty child."

Hecate waves her staff in a come-hither manner.

The ground near the merchant sparkles, and a moment later the two elves are transported close to us.

""*Sisters!*"""

The three girls catch their sisters.

"Ururu, Eruru, Oruru......"

"I never thought we'd see you again......"

They look frail but don't seem to have any injuries.

They wrap their arms weakly around their crying sisters.

"What?! What did you just do?!"

Having just lost his hostages, the merchant pitches forward and yells in shock.

"It can't have been?! Was that teleportation magic?! You can cast such advanced magic without a ritual?! Not even the court magicians can do something like that! Just who the heck......?!"

Hecate just laughs and doesn't answer.

"Urghhh......"

A thorough display of the difference in power.

Realizing that this time he's been cornered, the merchant drops his knife and falls to his knees.

"Give up. Time to confess all of your wrongdoings."

Keeping careful watch, Zenobia approaches the merchant.

"...I have my pride. And I will not allow myself to be captured..."

As the merchant's shoulders drop, he breaks something with a grunt.

He staggers to his feet.

"So you're still going to fight?"

"This isn't a fight...... It's suicide."

The merchant looks up with a dark light in his eyes, and before Zenobia can close the gap, he spits out an incantation.

The jewels on the collars around the necks of the docile monsters shatter immediately.

"Wh-what did you just do?!"

"If I'm going down, then I'm taking you bastards with me... At least I'll have completed my mission! We'll be overrun by hundreds of monsters! And you'll all die with me!"

As if in response to the merchant's broken laugh, the monsters in the cages begin to stir and emit low growls.

"E-eek?!"

Probably suffering a flashback, Drills starts freaking out.

Oh, right, this is like when we were back in her mansion.

The monsters start breaking out of their cages, fangs at the ready.

When crazed, these monsters will just attack anyone around them.

"Ha-ha-ha! Even you guys can't immediately defeat this many monsters! How many civilians will be slaughtered before all of these creatures are defeated?!"

Looks like if the merchant's going to lose, he's going to lose in style.

"You—you fiend!!"

"Call me whatever you want! It's already too late to kill me!! No one can stop this stampede!!"

Zenobia grits her teeth as the merchant crows.

"Arwf... *(Ummm...)*"

Sorry about this, you two.

I know I shouldn't ruin the scene, but we can handle this.

"Mew. *(Looks like it's your time to shine, Routa.)*"

"Squee. *(The man's a fool. Something like this is meaningless for my darling.)*"

"Arwf... *(Gimme a break...)*"

I step in front of the bloodshot eyes of the monsters and draw in a deep breath.

And as the monsters leap as one toward me, I pour all that air into one big howl.

"*Hoooooooowwwwwwwwl!! (All! Of! You! Siiiit!!)*"

My howl rings through the warehouse and drowns out the bellowing of the monsters and the crazed laugh of the merchant.

It is suddenly quiet enough to hear the walls falling apart, and all the monsters begin to grovel.

Each and every one of them is showing submission, trembling with their tails tucked between their legs.

"Arwf. *(Yes, that's a good beastie.)*"

This howl can make even the bravest of Fen Wolves clam up. No matter the monster, they always lose the will to fight and turn obedient.

Well, that's my job done. I'll leave the rest up to you guys.

"Wh-what the— What on earth just happened...?"

The merchant is looking around, dumbfounded, at the groveling monsters.

"Hi-ya!"

Zenobia sneaked in close to the merchant and now smashes him with her fist, sending him soaring into the air.

"Arwf. *(Damn, that was one hell of an uppercut.)*"

The merchant's body flies up and almost hits the ceiling.

Completely robbed of consciousness, his body hits the ground with a thud.

He is totally down for the count. Plan foiled again.

"Arwf! *(All of you, back to your crates! We'll be helping you soon, so behave.)*"

At my order, the monsters jump and start heading back to their cages.

"Wh-what did you do to us...?!"

The elves, who for some reason were with the rest of the monsters, have regained their sanity. They seem to be doing a lot better, probably because the influence of the collars has been cut off.

Zenobia nods in agreement and looks at me suspiciously.

"Routa, you really are..."

"Arwf?! *(Wait, seriously?!)*"

I've definitely used my power in front of Zenobia before this!

".........No. I've thought there was something mysterious about you since the very beginning. This doesn't surprise me. This time it's your victory. I'll not make little of it. You've done well. It's thanks to you that the Royal Capital has been saved."

Zenobia gives me an awkward pat on the head.

"A-arwf?! *(Zenobia's being magnanimous?! I can't believe it!)*"

Zenobia's just not herself without the whole "I don't trust you, beast! Grr, grr" thing.

"You're thinking something rude, aren't you…?!"

"Arwfrrr. *(N-no, no, of course not.)*"

"I'm only going to overlook this this once. If you ever turn your power on the young lady, I'll be ready for you."

"Woof, woof. *(Like I'd ever do that.)*"

Without Lady Mary, there'd be no lavish pet life to speak of. I'll continue serving her with all my heart. But I still don't plan on doing any real work.

Zenobia chuckles and rubs my head again, then goes to tie up the merchant.

"You really are the most amazing dog…"

Drills manages to make it all the way to the end without panicking. Looks like she's going to grow up to with a different sort of talent from Lady Mary.

And she somehow still thinks that I'm a dog! Talk about oblivious. Never change, Drills.

"But what's going to happen to these poor things? Maybe there are records or something of where they were caught. Maybe if they need a safe place to stay we could use my mansion…"

As she said that, Drills closed her eyes and shook her head.

"…No, I can't do that. It wouldn't be right to make them live somewhere they don't want to. I've already learned my lesson."

Well, that and the fact that they are monsters. They're playing nice right now because they're listening to me, but unless they're strange exceptions like Christina, they probably won't get along well with people.

"For now, I can testify to the evil actions of that man. And then,

once things quiet down, maybe I can come visit you? I did promise Mary that I would."

Sure thing, come visit whenever. We'll be glad to have you.

And maybe we can even sneak you out to visit the monsters that ran away from your mansion.

"U-ummm."

Swapping places with Drills, the five elf girls line up before me.

"They told us everything—that you're the one who saved us."

No, I didn't do that much. I just howled at the end; really Zenobia and Hecate did most of the work.

"Thank you so much for everything."

The elf who appears to be the oldest bows her head, and then the rest of the girls follow suit.

"Arwf, arwf. *(C'mon, that's enough of that.)*"

I'm just glad everything turned out all right.

"Arwf? *(But now what are you all going to do?)*"

The girls said that their village was gone and all their fellow villagers were scattered.

"I don't know… We could go back and rebuild our village, but who knows when people like that might come attack us again…"

"We don't really have anywhere to go."

"We had our hands full just trying to save our sisters."

"Guess we'll have to go back to getting by as burglars…"

No, no, no, that's a terrible idea. It would be a huge mistake to think that everyone is as nice as the people in my mansion. If you get caught, you might be sold right back into slavery.

"Oh my, perhaps I know of a place that you can go."

Hecate walks over, spinning her witch's hat on her finger.

"It's a place no one knows about, easy to live in, and surrounded by nature."

"A-a place like that would be…"

"Lady Luluarus! Please tell us where it is!"

"I suppose I could, but we'll have to ask the Lord of the Forest."

Hecate looks over at me.

Wait, me? I'm no lord. That forest is Papa's domain.

That said, Hecate has a point. With the Fen Wolves protecting it, that forest is as safe as can be.

Hecate lives there and she's also an elf, so it would be a great place to build a village. It's unbelievably huge, so it wouldn't matter if people did show up.

And if anything does happen, we're close enough to help.

"Arwf. *(I'm fine with it. I was planning on taking the monsters that wanted to go there back with me anyways.)*"

"Really?! Thank you so much!"

"You're so kind, my lord!"

"Thank you, my lord!"

The elves rush over and hug me.

Eh-heh-heh. No worries, no worries at all.

"Squeak squee-squeak! *(Hands off, you harlots! That's my husband! If you want to be his mistress, you better get in line!)*"

"D-did that mouse just talk......?!"

"Squeak!! *(I'm a dragon!!)*"

Please stop jumping around on top of my head.

"Now then, let's all teleport back. Nahura, your assistance, please."

"Mrow. *(Of course.)*"

And with that we can draw the curtain on tonight's excitement.

I still don't know entirely what the merchant was up to, but that's a job for someone greater than me. Whatever it is, it has nothing to do with a humble house pet like myself.

From the warehouse I can see the horizon and the sun just starting to peek above it.

Already morning. After everything that happened tonight, I'm exhausted. An afternoon nap sounds like the perfect plan for today.

Time to head home and sleep while my lady pets me.

It's been a while since the elves settled into living in the forest.

Thanks to the loan that Hecate got from Papa, the construction of their new village is coming along nicely. It also seems that they've been able to get in touch with some of their former friends, who've now come to join them.

They invited me over for a visit, but I should probably get them a housewarming gift before I go.

"Arwf. *(But learning that tall elf was the youngest of the group was one hell of a shock.)*"

The eldest's name is Aruru, and the next oldest is Iruru. After hearing that, I thought for a second that their names were decided by birth order, only to find out that it isn't some sort of elf custom. These are just childish names.

They talk the way they do so others don't look down on them. I guess there are people into the whole "older women acting immature" thing.

"Arwf, arwf! *(Anyway, let's see what's for breakfast today!)*"

I trot off to find the old man in the hope that a tasty morning meal awaits me.

"Ah, there you are."

Today's breakfast is a vegetable terrine.

A terrine is, roughly speaking, a Western-style jellied dish.

But it's completely different from the Japanese-style dish. Originally the word referred to a meal in which the ingredients were cooked in a terrine dish, but this doesn't look cooked at all.

A rectangular mold is lined with boiled cabbage, and then on top of that are layers of baby corn, asparagus, and zucchini. A thin gelatin solution made from a chicken-skin base is then poured over the whole thing.

Countless layers of vegetables and gelatin, vegetables and gelatin, until you reach the top, where the cabbage is wrapped over to form a cover.

It's then put in a cold place to cool, and once the gelatin sets, it's removed from the mold.

It looks just like a giant cabbage roll with angular corners, but once you cut into it you see the varied colors of the vegetables, and that's when you know you've got yourself a beautiful terrine.

Well, that's the gist of the explanation old man James was giving me as I ate.

"Awrmf wmf! *(These veggies are so good! And so sweet!)*"

"*Crunch, crunch. (Hmm, despite being heated completely through, the vegetables still maintain their crunch and haven't dissolved a bit. I really can't underestimate this human cooking.)*"

Len is right next to me, digging into the terrine.

The jelly filling the gaps between the vegetables results in an unusually thick umami flavor.

Just when it feels like the veggies aren't enough to satisfy your palate, a rich broth hits your tongue, almost as if you've taken a sip of a hearty soup.

"Garwf, arwf! *(Even though I prefer meat dishes, I can't get enough of this stuff!)*"

In my old life, I was the king of the unbalanced diet, but now I'll eat anything. As long as old man James is the one cooking, I'll take home the clean plate award every time.

"............"

As we're eating, he stares down at me. If he saw Len in her mouse form, it'd be a huge mess, so she's hiding away in my fur. He then mutters to himself.

"Done already?"

"Woof, woof! *(You bet! It was delicious!)*"

Tail wagging back and forth, I bark my thanks to old man James.

"Good, good, so now that you understand how precious these vegetables are, I've got a question for you."

The old man's slender yet incredibly sturdy arms reach out, and his hands grasp my face.

"Routa. Look me in the eyes and answer truthfully."

"Arwf?! *(Wha?! Why are you suddenly angry?!)*"

His intensity is as formidable as ever.

The more I've grown, the more ferocious my face has gotten, but the old man doesn't flinch from it one bit.

Even though I'm a bit bigger than he is, I'm fairly sure I'd be no match for him if he was truly pissed.

Chefs are terrifying...

"A-arwf, arwf?! *(Wh-wha-wha-wha-what's this all about?! Is this because I raided the cupboards? Or is this about me taking that piece of meat from the storeroom while it was still curing?! I'm the one who secured that meat in the first place, so that was just my fair share, wasn't it?! And it was still raw! I wasn't even the one who ate it! I gave it all to Garo and the wolves as thanks for watching over the elf village and taking care of all the monsters! They ate every last bite, including the bones! If you're mad about that, get mad at them! And Nahura and Len were there, too!)*"

"Squeak...... *(Darling, you're the worst......)*"

I hear Len's disgusted comment from behind me, but I ignore her.

This is a matter of life and death here.

Len can only say something like that because she's never been directly exposed to the old man's anger like this.

It's like being a fish on a cutting board. If I still had human sweat glands, I'd be soaked right now.

The old man is now uncomfortably close to me.

"You've gotten pretty large, haven't you? Yes, you look good enough to eat…"

What's he saying to himself?!

He's looking at me like he's picking out ingredients!

Oh, my lady. If the day comes that I suddenly vanish and you're served an unfamiliar meat for dinner, it's me. Please enjoy it, okay?

No, no, no, the old man would never do something like that.

…He wouldn't, right? He'd never cook me, the family's beloved pet, right?

I give the old man my best puppy-dog eyes.

"You wouldn't happen to know anything about the fields, would you?"

That's…not what I expected at all.

The old man pulls my face close and asks me something nonsensical.

"Arwf? *(Huh? The fields?)*"

What about 'em? I honestly have no idea where he's going with this.

My poaching territory is mainly the kitchen and the storeroom.

I don't even know where the fields are.

"Well, that response makes it obvious. Looks like you aren't the culprit."

"Arwf, arwf? *(What's up, old man? What happened to the fields?)*"

The old man's got his arms folded as he thinks, and I'm sitting in front of him, head tilted to the side.

"Welp, your nose might be of some use. Come with me."

"Woof? *(What are we doing?)*"

As the old man walks off, I follow him, utterly puzzled.

I guess I don't have any other plans.

If I did, they probably wouldn't involve much more than a postbreakfast nap, but falling under the old man's suspicions has me wide awake now.

And Lady Mary's morning classes haven't ended yet, so I don't have anyone to play with.

The family tutor is relatively strict and won't let me be there during classes, so we can only meet up during break and after classes are over.

And that won't be for another three hours.

Normally I'd be enjoying my midmorning nap right about now while waiting for Zenobia to come over to sneakily pet me (or try to attack me), but today I'll stick with the old man.

Lately I've been slipping away from the mansion at night, so that's been leaving me drowsy during the day.

"Squeak. *(You're always lazing about, darling. You're quite the deadbeat.)*"

"Arwf. *(Right back at you, deadbeat number two.)*"

Just for the record, deadbeat number three is Zenobia.

She's always patrolling the mansion, acting as security, but, too bad for her, there's no one trying to harm the family.

Though that might be because there's the King of the Fen Wolves here pretending to be a dog and a dragon pretending to be a mouse.

"Squeak. *(Hmm, well then, if we're both deadbeats, I guess that kind of makes us a couple, doesn't it?)*"

"Arwf. *(Nope.)*"

Instant denial.

But by that logic, wouldn't I be including Zenobia?

Zenobia in a wedding gown...that's a nice thought.

"Squeak. *(Tch. As cold as ever, darling... No matter; that's fine.)*"

Will you stop trying to trap me into commitment? Seriously, stop.

If I don't put my foot down with her, she immediately starts going on about marriage and babies.

"Okay, here we go."

The old man opens the rear gate and continues down the path.

At a fork in the road we take the path on the right and continue up a small hill until we get to an open area a few minutes down the road.

"Arwf...! *(Ohhh, these are the fields...!)*"

They're bigger than I thought.

A large number of vegetables are planted in neat rows. The variety is almost overwhelming.

It looks like there's enough here to feed everyone at the mansion and then some.

This must be where the veggies in my breakfast terrine came from.

And the old man takes care of all this by himself? What a legend.

"Well, what do you think? It's something, isn't it?"

"Woof, woof! *(This is amazing! You're amazing!)*"

Tail wagging, I sing the old man's praises.

"Neigh. *(Well now, if it isn't Mr. Wolf. We don't usually see you around here.)*"

"Arwf? *(Huh? Who was that?)*"

I turn in the direction of the horse's voice.

There's a wooden one-story bungalow standing near the fields. It's split into separate stalls, with a pair of horse heads sticking out.

These must be the stables where the horses live. And as you'd expect of the Faulks family stables, they're pretty impressive.

But why would these horses know me?

"Whinny? *(Come now, you're always riding behind us and you don't even know who we are?)*"

"Arwf? *(Hmm? ...Oh! Of course I do!)*"

They're the pair of horses who always pull the carriage whenever we go out to the lake.

But once we get to the lake, they always wait there patiently, so I never even considered the possibility that I could talk to them. I guess this body of mine can understand what regular animals say as well.

"Arwf, arwf? *(Why didn't you say anything earlier?)*"

"Whicker? *(Well, we couldn't chat while we're on the job, now, could we?)*"

Ah yes, the Faulks family horses, professionals through and through.

The stables are quite large and are divided into numerous stalls, but now these are the only two living here.

"Whicker. *(I guess this is the first time we've talked. I should introduce myself. My name's Elusive. And this is my wife, Grace.)*"

"Whinny. *(Nice to meet you, Mr. Wolf.)*"

The horse beside him gives a little whinny.

So they're a couple. The brown horse is Elusive and the gray horse is Grace. Okay, got it.

"Woof, woof. *(I'm Routa. And this little one is Len. Nice to meet you. Oh, and I'm not a wolf, I'm a dog. If you wouldn't mind.)*"

I plop before the lovely-coated horses and introduce myself.

"Woof. *(Thanks for all the work you do pulling the carriage! ... Sorry if my size makes that a bit difficult.)*"

"Neigh. *(Ha-ha-ha, you've definitely gotten heavier.)*"

"Whinny. *(And my husband and I are definitely getting up there in age, so it has been a bit more tiring recently.)*"

"Neigh. *(What are you saying, dear? I'm still in the prime of my life.)*"

"Whinny. *(We're old, honey. We're both over twenty years old now! The day we hang up our spurs is drawing ever closer.)*"

Twenty years is old for horses? I guess the large body comes with a reduced life span.

Speaking of, I wonder what my life expectancy is?

What's the average life span of a Fen Wolf, anyway? I'll have to ask Garo next time I see her.

"Squeak. *(Horses are certainly short-lived. That's not even one-fiftieth of my age.)*"

For her position atop my head, forearms crossed, Len gazes at the horses with pity.

"Woof. *(Well, of course it's different for spinsters.)*"

"Squeak?! *(Wh-who are you calling a spinster?! I'm still young! I'm a young maiden!)*"

"Arwf. *(Ha-ha-ha, don't forget to mention you're a thousand-year-old spinster.)*"

"Squeak! *(Quiet, you! Don't call me that!)*"

"Arwf! *(Ouch! Don't bite me!)*"

"Squeak, squeak! *(Darling, will you* please *let go of your reservations and commit yourself to me already?! Marry me! And then impregnate me!)*"

"Woof, woof! *(I said no! What do you think you're saying to a three-month-old puppy?!)*"

"Squeak! *(If we're in love, then age has nothing to do with it!)*"

"Woof, woof?! *(Well, what about the species difference?!)*"

"Squeak! *(That's why I learned how to turn into one of those humans you're so fond of!)*"

"Woof, woof! *(You were way too young! And that still doesn't solve the species difference!)*"

Rather than spending all that time on love and marriage, I'd rather just brainstorm more cute poses to get people to fawn over me.

"Hey! Routa! Catch up!"

Whoops, I got too caught up in the conversation.

Now the old man is all the way across the field.

"Arwf! *(See you later, you two. I'll come back sometime! Keep up the good work!)*"

Saying good-bye to the smiling Elusive and Grace, I hurry over to the old man.

† † †

"Awrooo… *(This is horrible…)*"

One row of vegetables has been completely torn up.

Piles of soil are scattered about, and nothing but empty holes adorn the carefully plowed row that should be richly populated by fresh veggies.

"This is it. This is where the carrots that I'd been raising so carefully should be…"

Ah, carrots.

In my past life I had a horribly unbalanced diet and didn't care much for vegetables, but now, thanks to the old man's cooking, I love them.

Now I just gobble them down.

His stewed carrots are so soft they almost melt, and the flavor is so deep and sweet that it's hard to believe he didn't add any sugar to the dish.

"Sorry I suspected you. I didn't really think you were the culprit, but I had to make sure."

"Arwf. *(No worries. If my field were destroyed like this, I'd be pissed, too.)*"

Watering them every day. Picking bugs off the leaves. Pulling weeds and laying out fertilizer.

Farming is hard work.

Even an amateur like me knows that.

I have only the deepest respect for someone who maintains the fields while working as a chef.

Talking about thieves makes me think of our burglar elf friends, but they wouldn't do something like this. Plus, they said something about a rule to only steal from bad people.

They should be living peacefully and building their village in the forest. And any current food needs should be covered by the funds Papa gave them. They don't have any reason to steal food.

"So then."

"Arwf? *(Yes?)*"

Now old man James is smirking.

"I want to know who stole these carrots. And of course, this affects your food stores as well. So we should be working together, right?"

"Arwf? *(Eh?)*"

"We'll. Work. Together. Right?"

He draws closer to me with every word.

His smile gets closer. And scarier.

"A-arwf! *(J-just leave it to me!)*"

There wasn't anything I could do but spit out an answer.

What the heck?!

I just want to get back to my lazy dog life of eating and sleeping!

But it seems things are getting crazy again!

"Okay then, I'm counting on you!"

And with that, old man James went back home.

Leaving behind his pitifully destroyed field, a dog (not really), and a mouse (also not really).

I don't really want to work, but I am a bit concerned about the case of the old man's missing veggies.

Now that I've learned the wonders of vegetables, I can't imagine life without them.

So I guess I'll have to put forth a little effort in order to catch our vegetable thief.

"Squeak? *(Darling, he said to search for the culprit, but how should we go about it?)*"

"Woof. *(If we're conducting an investigation, we gotta start by interviewing witnesses.)*"

What's going to solve this case won't be some detective reasoning but good ol'-fashioned police work.

Just like a buddy cop show. No doubt.

And I know just the pair to question.

There should be some witnesses right nearby.

"Woof, woof! *(Hey, you two!)*"

"Neigh. *(Well, if it isn't Routa. Back already?)*"

Back at the stables I give a rundown of the situation to Elusive and Grace.

I tell them about the torn-up carrot patch and how the old man left the investigation to me.

"Whinny. *(Well, we knew about the carrot patch being destroyed. Mr. James was yelling about it this morning.)*"

I can easily picture the old man yelling, "What the hell is thiiis?!"

"Squeak? *(And when was that?)*"

"Neigh. *(That was at daybreak. His yelling actually woke us up. And there wasn't anyone here until at least as late as we went to bed last night.)*"

Which means our culprit was here sometime during the night.

"Squeak? *(And of course you two aren't responsible, right?)*"

"Neigh. *(Of course not. We'd have no reason to steal vegetables. We're always properly fed.)*"

"Whinny. *(Certainly we eat some carrots, but only the ones that have been culled for being too thin. Though they're still very tasty.)*"

"Whinny. *(We have a long history of serving the Faulks family. We would never pilfer food. That would be very poor manners.)*"

Okay. That's enough. That's starting to cut a little deep.

Welp, I don't have a long history as the Faulks family pet. And I've definitely stolen food. I'm sorry.

But when I'm hungry I've got no choice.

With this growing body of mine, three meals a day plus snacks just isn't enough.

Plus, Nahura and Len were right there eating next to me.

Len doesn't eat a lot, but Nahura eats so much it makes you wonder where she's putting it all.

Another mystery for the formerly dead homunculus.

"Squeak. *(Of course. I had to ask, but I apologize for making it seem like we suspected you.)*"

Len offers a polite apology to the couple professing their innocence.

She may be proud, but thankfully she's not arrogant.

She'll admit her mistakes and is kind to basically everyone.

If she weren't an ancient, cradle-robbing dragon, she'd actually be prime wife material.

Unfortunately, her negatives greatly outweigh her positives. Poor thing.

"Arwf. *(Looks like our investigation was a bust. Guess we'll have to go back to check out the scene of the crime.)*"

Time for this super-wolf body of mine to be put to work.

† † †

Sniff sniff.

Ah, *sniff sniff.*

My nose is buried in the ravaged vegetable patch as I try to sniff out a scent.

"Squeak? *(Well? Have you found anything?)*" Len asks from atop my head, her tiny eyes staring into mine.

"Arwf! *(Oh! I got something!)*"

"Squeak! *(I always believed in you, darling! What is it?)*"

"Arwf! *(I've found out that I haven't found anything!)*"

"Squeak? *(......Do you* want *me to bite you?)*"

"A-arwf, arwf! *(W-wait, wait! It was a joke! And look, maybe we don't need a scent to follow.)*"

Looking carefully next to the empty row of vegetables, I see a set of footprints.

The footprints are U-shaped, so I guess *hoofprints* would be more accurate.

And they're also clearly much larger than anything that would be left by Elusive or Grace.

"Squeak? *(Do you think a wild horse got in somehow?)*"

"Arwf. *(Looks like that may be the case.)*"

Garo and the Fen Wolves only hunt monsters that do harm to the forest, so it wouldn't really surprise me if wild horses also live in there somewhere.

"Arwf. *(Well, I guess we should follow the tracks.)*"

Whoever made these hoofprints didn't use the path after

eating the carrots and destroying the field but headed straight back toward the forest.

But from what I can tell of the hoofprints, our target should be huge, and the prints are oddly shallow.

If it was a giant horse, I'd expect these hoofprints to be a lot deeper...

Following the tracks, I step into the forest.

Because the area is so densely wooded, even with the sun up, it's still remarkably dim.

The tracks continue deeper inside, and I continue following them.

"Arwf... (Hmm...)"

As the forest opens up into a small clearing, I come to a halt.

This clearing is the only spot in the forest that receives full sunlight.

"Squeak? (What is it, darling? Why did you stop?)"

"Woof. (The tracks disappeared.)"

"Squeak? (They've disappeared?)"

"Woof. (Yep, they just...stop here.)"

They vanish without a trace.

The scent is gone, too.

All traces of our culprit are gone, as though they never existed.

"Bark. (Now, don't get scared.)"

I thought we were playing detective, but without realizing it, I've become the star of my own horror movie, and an indescribable fear has my hackles on edge.

A ghost. This is the sign of a ghost.

And what's even more terrifying is that ghosts might be a regular occurrence in this fantasy world.

"Arwf. (Hey, Len.)"

"Squeak? (What is it?)"

"Arwf. (Let's get out of here.)"

"Squeak? (Whatever for?)"

"Arwf? (What, you can't tell? Obviously because this is terrifying.)"

This is one of my faults.

When it comes to horror, I'm no good with gore, but ghosts and ghouls are just as bad.

"Squeak? *(How can you say that with such confidence? …Sigh, how pitiful. You're King of the Fen Wolves, and without even knowing what you're facing, you're going to turn tail and run. And yet you managed to defeat me…)*"

"Woof. *(Okay, well, you can stay here. We don't know when our culprit will be back, after all.)*"

"S-squeak?! *(Wh-what?!)*"

"Woof. *(If you're not scared, that's fine. But this pitiful little puppy is going home. My bed awaits.)*"

"S-squeak! *(Y-you'd leave a defenseless maiden alone in a place like this?! You're the worst! Of course I'd be scared if I was left alone here!)*"

"Woof, woof?! *(Weak?! You're a dragon!! And you're no maiden, you're a hag! A thousand-year-old spinster!)*"

"Squeak, squeak! *(Quiet, you! I told you not to call me that! It sounds so horribly unpleasant!)*"

After arguing the whole way home, we decide to take another stab at the investigation that evening with Nahura in tow.

I-it's not just because we thought it would be too spooky at night and wanted the extra company. Definitely not.

"Mrow? *(A ghost?)*"

"Woof. *(Yes.)*"

"Squeak. *(Exactly.)*"

At midnight we met up with Nahura and explained the field situation to her.

We told her about the torn-up carrot patch, the mysterious hoofprints, and following those tracks into the forest, where they suddenly vanished into thin air.

As she listened to our fears, Nahura began snickering.

"Mew. *(I can't believe it. You two actually believe in ghosts? Of course ghosts aren't real. Pfft.)*"

"Woof! *(Hey!)*"

"Squeak! *(Hey!)*"

Seeing Nahura raise her paws to her face in an attempt to hide a big Cheshire grin is really pissing me off.

"Woof? *(Aren't you practically a ghost yourself, Ms. Former Corpse?)*"

"Squeak? *(What's that? I haven't heard this story.)*"

"Mew, mew. *(I'm a homunculus made from the corpse of a cat. I'm a high-performance familiar that my mistress made by bringing together the genius of various scholars. Please don't lump me in with ghosts, which have no scientific basis at all.)*"

"S-squeak! *(Th-that's incredible!)*"

Len's showering Nahura with praise while Nahura puffs her chest out with pride.

With all the magic she's been flinging around, I wonder what Len thought Nahura was? Just a regular gluttonous, alcoholic, worthless cat? Well, I guess that's not too far off.

"Woof. *(Anyway, tonight we're keeping watch in the fields. Let's go.)*"

And with that, I set off toward our destination.

Len and Nahura both settle down on my back.

"Bark. *(Hey, you two do have legs, you know.)*"

"Mewl. *(Oh, but Routa, your back is just so comfortable.)*"

"Squeak. *(And it's not like we weigh that much, so stop complaining. What do you have to complain about with two beautiful women on top of you?)*"

Maybe the fact that you're both animals?

I'll say it again for emphasis. You are both *animals*!

And "beautiful"? If we were strangers, I wouldn't even know if you were guys or girls.

Also, I bet Nahura hasn't taken a bath recently, because she smells wild.

What do you think will happen to me if I go back to my lady's bed smelling like an animal?

And, bickering as we always do, the three of us head off to the fields.

Looks like Elusive and Grace have already retired for the night.

The quiet stable is dimly lit by an ore lamp.

We quietly creep past the stables, so as not to disturb the sleeping horses, and settle into a patch of grass near the fields.

"Woof. *(Your turn, Nahura.)*"

"Mew? *(What?)*"

"Woof. *(I'm leaving the next shift to you. I'm going to sleep.)*"

"Squeak. *(Well then, I'll sleep as well. If you see anything, do let us know, Nahura.)*"

"M-mew?! *(Wh-what?! That's not fair!)*"

Don't both of you eat and sleep more than me during the day?

Meanwhile, I'm busy playing with my lady, assisting the old man with odd jobs, and helping Toa the twin-tailed maid hang up the laundry.

It's time for me to make up for my chronic sleep deprivation.

"Mew... *(You're all too familiar with working this familiar to death...)*"

Familiar with working a familiar? That's a new one.

"Mew! *(Ah! Routa, Routa!)*"

"Arwf?! *(What?! Are they already here?!)*"

I raise my head from my paws.

"Mew! *(Look! Look at this weird bug!)*"

"Woof, woof! *(Don't interrupt my sleep for something like that!)*"

Nahura's got something that looks like a rhinoceros beetle caught between her front paws.

I rearrange myself and try to settle back down to sleep.

"Squeak! *(Darling! Darling!)*"

"Arwf? *(Come on now. Is this just another weird bug?)*"

"Squeak! *(That's not it! It's here! Our thief!)*"

Looking in the direction Len is pointing from her place atop my head, I see a flickering firelight approaching the fields.

"Arwf…? *(A torch? Does that mean our thief is a human?)*"

There aren't any villages nearby, so whoever it is has to have purposefully come out this far.

All to steal the family's vegetables. What a jackass.

I think it's time to give them a bit of a scare with my trusty wolf face.

Without a sound I dash over toward the flickering torchlight.

"Grwwl, grwwl! *(Hey, you! This is my turf! No trespassing! Get outta here! And don't come back!)*"

I jump into the torchlight, where I can be seen, and give a mighty howl.

"Ar-ar-ar-arooo?! *(What's the matter?! Too scared to speak?!)*"

Well, this would be a shock.

If a giant wolf suddenly appeared in front of me like this, I'm sure I'd faint in an instant.

And, of course, piss myself.

"…………"

I'm realizing that whoever is holding this torch is way too quiet.

Did they really just faint standing up?

I've been so focused on the flame that I didn't get a good look at the person carrying it.

Squinting as hard as I can, I take a good look at them.

"Arwf……? *(Hmm……?)*"

That's…not a person.

It's a horse. A horse is here.

But it's no ordinary horse.

Its mane and tail are alight with a spectral flame, and its eyes shine bloodred.

From their lofty position, the rectangular pupils look down at me. The moment our eyes meet, the flames of its mane flare up violently.

The force of the flames is so strong that the hide of the burning horse appears transparent in its light.

But beneath the hide isn't muscle—just bare, fleshless bones.

In the face of this terrifying sight, only one reaction seems appropriate—

"Ee-eeeek!! *(A-a ghost!!)*"

Without thinking, I grab Nahura from my back and hold her in front of me as a shield.

"Meeeeww!! *(N-nooooooo!!)*"

The moment I grab Nahura, she, in turn, grabs Len and shoves her forward.

"Squeeeeak!! *(Wait, don't do it!!)*"

Having nothing to shield herself with, Len just screams at the burning skeletal horse.

Seeing this, the horse, who was frozen until Len screamed, rears up, half-crazed, on its hind legs.

"Neeeeeeeeigh!! *(A-a ghost?! I hate ghosts!!)*"

""""WoofMrowSqueak!! *(We're talking about youuuuuu!!)*"""""

The cries of four animals ring across the darkened fields.

✝ ✝ ✝

"Neigh?! Neeeeeeigh?! *(A ghost?! Where's the ghost?!)*"

The occasionally transparent burning horse is still panicking, whinnying, rearing, and foaming at the mouth.

""""   . . . .   """""

Meanwhile, we've calmed down and continue to watch it.

It's a classic example of the phenomenon whereby you get really calm after seeing someone else freaking out a little too much.

This guy is a legit ghost, and yet I'm not scared at all. It's probably because he's a total coward. I just can't see him doing anything evil.

This goes on for a minute or so before finally the horse's panic starts to subside.

"Wh-whinny…? *(…Ummm, where's the ghost…?)*"

Now that it finally realizes things have calmed down, the intensity of the horse's flames begins to lessen, but it still seems uncertain.

"Woof. *(Well, we thought that you were the ghost.)*"

"N-neeeeeigh?! *(A-a wolf?!)*"

"Woof?! *(You just noticed that?!)*"

Whatever, just please calm down.

"Whinny! *(Don't eat me! Please don't eat me!)*"

I'm not going to eat you.

I'm a pampered pooch. I only eat cooked meat.

That being said, horse sashimi is delicious…

Especially with some thick, sweet soy sauce and a bit of grated ginger.

And after your tongue is coated with the fat of the meat, you wash it down with a swig of dry shochu on the rocks…

"…*Drool. (Whoops, I'm drooling.)*"

"Neeeeigh!! *(N-noooooooo!! I knew it! You are going to eat meeee!!)*"

"Woof, woof. *(Oh shoot, I'm sorry. I'm not going to eat you, please calm down.)*"

I try to calm the horse as it starts to get worked up again.

"Squeak? *(Say, darling, isn't this our thief? Why don't we just end this with me eating it? I could change back, and it would only take one bite.)*"

"Woof. *(Don't say disturbing things like that. It's innocent until proven guilty. And I just promised it that we wouldn't eat it, so let's hear what it has to say first.)*"

And old man James did say he just wanted to know who the culprit was.

He didn't say anything about capturing or punishing them.

This horse may look terrifying, but it talks normally. Once it calms down and explains what's going on, we might understand the situation.

If it doesn't settle down, we can't do anything.

We wait for the horse's panic to subside.

But something's off. If it's this scared, why didn't it just run off?

More patient waiting.

Len curls up on my head, and Nahura starts grooming herself.

And so we wait for a while again.

"Wh-whinny *(U-ummm...... I'm sorry. I just, I get startled easily......)*"

Speaking hesitantly, the horse has finally calmed down once again.

"Bark. *(We're not going to attack you; don't be so worried.)*"

"Neigh... *(But you were just drooling, Mr. Wolf... And that mouse, it blatantly said it was going to eat me...)*"

"Squeak. *(I'm not a mouse. I'm an elder dragon,)*" Len boasts as she stands.

"Wh-whinny?! *(A-a dragon?! Dragons are scary!!)*"

Not again.

We just started talking. Could you not interrupt, please?

I give my head a shake to dislodge Len.

Right toward where Nahura is sitting at the base of my tail.

"Mew. *(Well, hello there.)*"

Nahura snags Len out of the air.

This guy's the type to be afraid of mice, so it'll be best to simply hide Len for now.

Though I think a dragon is way scarier than a mouse.

"Squeak! *(Hey! You two have been very rude toward me recently!)*"

Don't worry, there's nothing "recent" about it. We've been treating you like this from the very beginning.

I ignore Len's squeaking protest, coming from where she's trapped, in Nahura's front paws.

I need to keep the horse talking.

"Woof, woof. *(I'm Routa. I'm not a wolf; I'm a dog. This cat is Nahura. And Lenowyrm over there is a mouse who thinks she's a dragon.)*"

"Squeak, squeak?! *(What?! What do you mean 'thinks'?! I am a dragon! I'm a real dragon!)*"

"Arwf. *(She's a little touched in the head. Forgive her.)*"

"Neigh... *(Ohhh, poor thing...)*"

The horse gives Len a look full of pity.

"Squeak! *(Listen to me!)*"

"Mew. *(Please calm down, Lady Len. There, there.)*"

The furious Len is trying to struggle out of Nahura's grasp.

She could easily prove herself by revealing her dragon form, but we're too close to the mansion.

Figuring this was going to turn into a troublesome situation, I told Len to refrain from transforming before we got out here.

As soon as I hammered home the point that she'd never get to taste the old man's cooking again if she was discovered, she immediately acquiesced.

Thus, she can't turn into a dragon. So she should just calm down and wait patiently.

"Whinny... *(Poor little mouse...)*"

"Squeak?! *(You're pitying me?!)*"

The shock at being pitied by this horse shows all over Len's face.

"Squeak... *(B-but I am a dragon... I really am... I'm not just saying things...)*"

"Mewl. *(Shh. Stop interrupting the conversation, Lady Len. Would you like some cheese?)*"

"Squeak... *(Sniffle... Yes, please...)*"

Nahura retrieves a piece of cheese from parts unknown and gives it to Len.

Len's nose is trembling, and she looks on the verge of tears.

This elder spinster dragon really has low mental fortitude.

Now that the person who was interrupting the conversation is quiet, I turn back to the horse.

"Woof? *(So what's your deal? You don't look like an ordinary horse.)*"

"Neigh?! *(Huh? I'm a horse?!)*"

"Arwf?! *(Seriously?!)*"

Another case of having to start with explaining what someone is.

How can this horse not know it's a horse?

Oh, actually, I guess I'm the same way.

I'm a giant wolf pretending to be a dog.

Guess I don't have a leg to stand on.

"Whinny... *(I see. So I'm a horse... No wonder I like carrots so much...)*"

Well, that was incriminating. Looks like we've found our culprit.

But the more I talk to it, the less it seems like some evil monster.

It's way different from those evil goblins or that angry boar I fought before.

Its outward form is larger than any standard horse's, but it seems to have the mind of a child.

"Whinny... *(I-I'm sorry. I really can't remember anything...)*"

"Bark? *(You can't remember anything? Like amnesia?)*"

Amnesia strong enough to make you forget you're a horse—wow.

Maybe that childishness stems from a lack of memories.

"Neigh. *(I was starving and wandering through the forest when I smelled something delicious... I didn't know they belonged to you. I'm sorry.)*"

"Woof. *(Well, they're not really ours. But you're causing trouble for the person who manages these fields, so you can't just go off eating things.)*"

I get that this horse isn't a bad guy, but what am I supposed to do with a giant amnesiac monster horse?

I'm sure that if I introduced him to the old man, he'd apologize, but if old man James saw a horse that's clearly a monster of some sort, he'd die of shock.

......Or would he?

He might just look at him as a meal and be glad for the generous portions.

Old man James is definitely the scariest one among us.

Not to mention that in order to protect my peaceful pet life, I need everyone in the mansion to keep believing that this is a pleasant area without a single monster living in the forest.

So it's not as simple as just sending this guy back to the forest.

"Squeak— *(Which is why I said the fastest way to deal with this is—)*"

"Woof. *(And I said we're not doing that.)*"

As always, Len's proposed retribution goes way overboard.

She's kind to friends but has no sympathy for enemies. I guess that's part of being a dragon.

But eating someone just because they ate some carrots is taking it too far.

I may have to teach Len how to be a pet again.

"Woof? *(Len, Nahura, does either of you have any idea what species of monster this guy is?)*"

"Squeak? *(Ummm… Some sort of…burning horse?)*"

"Mew. *(Well, he's clearly a type of spirit, but I don't know the specific species. I expect Mistress would know.)*"

"Woof. *(Ah, that's true. Let's ask Hecate.)*"

I forgot about our neighborhood witch of many talents.

She's the one person who knows all our true forms and situations and will probably lend a hand if we ask.

"Mew… *(No, actually, Mistress has been extraordinarily busy…)*"

"Woof? *(Oh, really?)*"

I guess the guild's keeping her busy, what with the whole mess with the elves and the slave trader.

Nahura gives an evasive answer.

"Mew. *(Recently, she's been holed up in her workshop. She even ordered me not to contact her telepathically.)*"

"Bark… *(Well, if she's that busy, we…we probably shouldn't bother her…)*"

Speaking of, I haven't seen her even once since we came back from our trip to the city.

I should invite her to come over once she's free again. We're friends, after all. And Lady Mary would love to see her.

I'm really interested in whatever she's got going on that has her locked away in her workshop.

But right now, we've got to deal with this horse.

And it's looking like we're going to have to do it ourselves.

"Grr…? *(What're we gonna do with you…?)*"

As I mull over the possibilities, the horse suddenly falls over with a thud.

"W-woof *(Wh-what are you doing?)*"

"N-neigh… *(I'm just so hungry…)*"

Hungry enough to collapse?

But I can't let it eat what's in the fields, and I guess the leaves around us are no good.

"Neigh! *(Hey, Routa!)*"

"Whinny! *(Bring that little one over here!)*"

The sound of whinnying comes from the stables.

It's Elusive and Grace. The uproar earlier must have woken them up.

"Woof, woof. *(Come on, get up, horse. Some other horses—though I guess* other *doesn't really apply in this situation—are calling us.)*"

"Neigh… *(Okay…)*"

Elusive and Grace have been helping us with this whole investigation. This will at least be a temporary solution as we tell them what we've discovered.

I just hope they aren't too surprised when they see this giant, burning, see-through horse.

As I lead the swaying horse into the barn, Elusive sticks his head out of his stall.

"Whinny. *(Go ahead and eat some of this fodder.)*"

Elusive grabs a chunk of grass wrapped in netting from the wall and passes it over.

"Woof? *(Are you sure? Isn't this your portion?)*"

"Whinny. *(We've both had our fill. It'll get replenished tomorrow anyway.)*"

I offer thanks to the pair and then drop the feed in front of the burning horse.

"Woof. *(Lucky you. Um…by the way, I don't suppose you know your own name?)*"

"N-neigh! *(F-food! Food!)*"

"Woof! *(Pay attention!)*"

The horse has shoved its head into the feed bag and begins wolf-ing down the contents.

"*Munch munch! (This is delicious! So good! Thank you, mister! Thank you, ma'am!)*"

"Whinny. *(That's all well and good, but do slow down.)*"

"Whinny. *(Don't worry; that's all for you. So take your time and enjoy it.)*"

Elusive is looking a little nervous about the situation, while Grace is looking at the new horse with kindness in her eyes.

I'm a bit worried myself that the flames from the horse's tail are going to spread to the barn.

The couple seems to be taking this all pretty well. More of that obliviousness? I guess they are members of the Faulks family.

"Mew? *(What was that, Routa?)*"

Nahura, who resumed grooming herself as the horse fixated on eating, lifts her head.

"Arwf? *(Huh? I didn't say anything. Did you, Len?)*"

"Squeak. *(Wasn't me... This feed isn't very good. Not to my taste at all.)*"

Len throws away the piece of feed she's been nibbling at.

"Bark? *(Maybe you were just hearing things?)*"

"Mew. *(It must have come from outside. I swear I heard what sounded like someone talking.)*"

Huh? Maybe it's the old man?

Whether it's him or someone else from the mansion, we can't let them see this crazy horse.

"Woof! *(Nahura, Len, I'll go buy some time. You two do something to hide this horse!)*"

"Mew? *(What? How do you expect us to do that?!)*"

"Squeak? *(Can't we just use your spatial magic?)*"

"Mew! *(Ohhh, nice idea, Lady Len. Very clever!)*"

"Squeak. *(Exactly. I am very clever.)*"

Nahura sings her praises, and Len's head swells.

Despite my anxiousness, I go flying out of the barn to buy us some time.

"Arwf! *(Hey, I don't know who's out there, but try to resist my adorable pose!)*"

Whether it's the old man or one of the maids, come at me!

I tuck into a front roll, flipping over onto my back and ending in a full-body pet-me pose.

"Ha-ha-ha... *(Come on, aren't I cute?! Pet me, rub me! Come on! ...Wait, what?)*"

There's no response to my adorable display.

And there's no one coming from the direction of the mansion.

Instead there's a human figure, covered in a tattered cloak, limping its way out of the forest.

"I've found you... Nightmare... Why would you run from our master to come to a place like this...?"

It's a gloomy voice that sounds like it comes straight from a deep, dark abyss.

"A-arwf?! *(Who are you?! And who's Nightmare?! There's no one like that here!)*"

"...Reveal yourself, Nightmare..."

The cloak-covered figure ignores me and raises what it's carrying.

In its hand is a giant scythe.

The handle is long, and the blade is huge. It has an ominous shape, as though it could reap human souls as easily as stalks of rice.

And at the same time, I see the face lurking below the figure's hood.

It's a skull.

No muscle, no flesh—just a terrifying skull.

"E-eeeek?! *(Another ghost appeared?!)*"

Due to the sheer terror of the sight, I piss myself while in my submissive pose.

The yellow liquid sketches a parabolic arc in the air, coming down to land on the cloak of the skeleton.

The warm fluid soaks into the cloak.

"A-arwf. *(Ahhh, my bad.)*"

"......Die."

The skeleton doesn't hesitate.

Scythe raised high over my belly, the skeleton ruthlessly swings it downward, splitting it right in two.

The scythe, that is.

The giant blade spins off with a hum.

The scythe blade, which was expected to tear into my exposed stomach, snapped off at the hilt and vanished into the tall grass.

"................What...?"

The skeleton is staring at its scythe handle, dumbfounded, and my urine goes back to soaking its robe.

Did you know?

Big dogs pee for a really long time. Sometimes they take minutes.

And I'm a giant wolf, larger than a small cow.

It's like a hose with the water pressure on full blast.

It just keeps coming and coming.

My lukewarm stream relentlessly seeps into the skeleton's cloak.

The now mildly drenched cloak is sticking to the bones, revealing the thin frame of the skeleton.

While peeing, I couldn't help but think how uncomfortable this must be if the bones have nerves in them.

"Arwf... *(That's... It's just... I'm so sorry.)*"

As I try to apologize again, the sound of laughter floats out of the stables.

"Mrow! *(Pffft! Peeing on someone as soon as you meet them! How many more times are you going to do that? Ha-ha-ha-ha-ha!)*"

Nahura is rolling around in stitches, paws clasped to her stomach.

"Squeak. *(Ha-ha-ha, how magnificent. That's just like you, darling!)*"

Why is Len laughing about this?

She's bragging like she did it herself.

"Squeak. *(Mr. Skull, I apologize on behalf on my darling.)*"

With a cheerful laugh, Len calls out to the skeleton.

But then her eyes narrow.

"Squeak. (... *That said, for the crime of raising that blade, the sentence is death.)*"

As soon as she says this with a cold, ruthless voice, Len's small tail becomes massive in an instant.

The tail is long and thick like a steel whip and is clad in giant scales.

Only her tail reverted to dragon form—or, rather, shed its mouse form.

The tail is so large compared to her mouse body that it looks like it's springing directly out of the ground.

Wouldn't the weight of the tail crush the body?

As I'm puzzling over this, the giant tail accelerates into a blur.

"Squeak. *(Repent of your sins and die.)*"

There isn't a chance to stop her.

The swinging dragon tail breaks the sound barrier, flashes over me, and smashes sideways through the skeleton.

With a dry *poof* the skeleton explodes, spreading bone dust across the night sky.

It's been smashed into smithereens.

The extreme scale and speed of that attack completely removed any existence of the skeleton.

And the terror of such an attack whistling over my head has finally stilled my peeing.

And caused my balls to retract.

"Squeak. *(Hmph, how vulgar. Swinging a blade at my darling? Unforgivable.)*"

Breathing heavily, Len declares her victory.

Y-yaaay...

I can really feel Len's love for me.

It's so strong.

I'm so happy.

Blech.

I can't do anything but give a wry laugh.

"Squeak. *(See, darling? If anyone ever tries to harm you, I will destroy them completely and utterly.)*"

"A-arwf. *(Th-Thanks. You saved me. But we're still not a couple, okay? Can you stop trying to get that established as a fact?)*"

She may be mentally weak, but physically she's top class.

I better do everything in my power to stay on her good side.

I really don't want to see her lovesick-to-the-point-of-violence side, so maybe it's time to hold off on teasing her for a while.

"......Futile......"

We hear the voice of the supposedly dead skeleton.

"This body was given to me by the Ruler of the Dead... So long as it retains his magic...I will continue to be restored..."

Who's this Ruler of the Dead?

Another person I've never heard of.

No, wait, I feel like I have heard that name before.

Wasn't it in that book my lady was reading?

The source of the information aside, if this guy is the minion of that Ruler of the Dead guy, does he really have infinite lives?

But as he said, he's starting to re-form from the feet up.

That's one heck of a rebuild time. It looks like even the scythe is being re-formed.

At this pace he'll be back in a matter of seconds.

"Woof, woof?! *(What do we do?! What do we do?! Limitless respawns is a total cheat! This guy's cheating!)*"

"Heh-heh-heh... I'll not fail again. I shall reap all of your souls..."

The half-rebuilt skull of the skeleton rattles and laughs.

"Squeak. *(Hmph, is that so? Then try this on for size.)*"

The skeleton is hammered again by the merciless dragon tail.

With a smashing sound, the skeleton is flattened into the ground.

"A-arwf? *(Eh, um, wait, Len?)*"

Len's remorseless attack without consideration for the situation has me trembling.

I mean, the skeleton was just starting his monologue.

Don't you have the decency to let him finish?!

"F-futile……"

Just as the powdered bones start to re-form, the dragon tail smashes them from above again.

"F-futile……"

Smash.

"Futi……"

Crunch.

"Fu……"

Whomp.

"…………"

Shatter.

Crash. Thwack.

Smash. Crunch. Whomp. Shatter.

Wallop. Crash. Thwack. Thrash. Crunch. Smash.

As if she were hammering a nail into a piece of wood, Len continues to flatten the skeleton.

How many minutes have passed?

I can't even hear the groans of the skeleton now.

Len lifts her tail from the depression in the ground.

The remnants are so mixed in with the soil that I can't tell what is and isn't bone anymore.

"Squeak. *(Hmph, that was easy.)*"

"A-arwf… *(I—I don't think it's moving anymore…)*"

"Squeak, squeak. *(It said it couldn't die so long as it had magic remaining, which means that there's a limit. So if it doesn't die, I just have to keep killing it until it does.)*"

Well…that's one way to get the job done.

Len's scary.

I normally only see her weepy mouse form, but she's actually terrifying.

"Woof? *(But what did he want? I'm assuming the Nightmare he mentioned was that idiot horse. And who's this Ruler of the Dead guy?)*"

There are too many monsters in this forest.

And for a thousand years, none of them leaked out.

The Fen Wolves are way too efficient.

"Arwf... *(Hmm, Ruler of the Dead...)*"

That definitely sounds like the name of a boss character.

If there's someone in there like that, I'm sure Garo and the other wolves will take care of it.

I should go ask them about it. They're the best source of info about the forest.

This was just supposed to be about finding whoever was raiding the fields, but I think it's turning into something much larger.

"Woof... *(No, no, this is all for my comfortable, slacker dog life. I just have to work a bit harder...)*"

I could worry myself sick about the contradiction of working for the sake of not working, but I think I'll just ignore it instead.

I already experienced all that back when I was a wage slave!

I don't wanna relive those dark days!

"Mew? *(But, Routa, isn't that putting the cart before the horse?)*"

"Bark! *(Don't say it! Let me have my delusions!)*"

And to the familiar tune of our bickering, the spatial magic whisks us away to pick up our horse.

"Bark! *(Thus, this is our veggie pilferer!)*"

"Whinny! *(I'm sorry! I'm sorry! I'm sorry!)*"

The following morning, I turn the horse Nightmare over to old man James.

"Hmm? So this is the culprit?"

The old man, who has come to join us in the fields, crosses his arms and raises an eyebrow.

"Wow. Well, he certainly is a big fella, isn't he?"

My lady, who tagged along from the mansion, looks up at the pitch-black body of the nightmare.

Now, as to why the two of them aren't afraid of Nightmare, a flaming skeletal horse, we'll have to go back to last night.

† † †

"Woof, woof? *(Okay, now that we've defeated that grim reaper–like skeleton, how about we go find that stupid horse?)*"

After all that, we still don't know much about whatever that skeleton was.

He came looking for the horse, but they really didn't seem like buddies. He was way more evil than the horse, after all.

Oh well, even if we did want to question him, he's now mixed in the earth near the fields with my pee.

"Woof, woof? *(By the way, where did you send the horse?)*"

Hopefully he's safe. Wherever he is, he's probably panicking at being transported there without explanation.

Oh yeah, I guess he's Nightmare. I remember the skeleton calling him that.

Although I don't know if that's a species name or a given name.

"Mew. *(I only have three set anchors—the workshop, you, and the hot spring—so I sent him to the hot spring.)*"

"Bark. *(Hecate would kill you if you sent him to the workshop out of the blue. Wait, you still have an anchor attached to me...?)*"

It is convenient to have instant access.

But I wouldn't mind *not* having this infringement on my privacy.

"Meow. *(Well then, let's teleport over.)*"

"Bark. *(All right, then.)*"

"Squee. *(If you would.)*"

As Nahura uses her teleportation magic, everything goes white, and we appear on the riverbed.

A small river runs through the middle of the deep forest. The nearby dug-out hot spring still seems to be working, and steam and the sound of rushing water hang in the air.

"Woof, woof! *(Hey! Horse! Nightmare! Where are you?!)*"

"Neigh! *(I'm over here!)*"

Following the sound of the reply, we find the horse submerged in the hot spring.

Lying down, eyes closed, with his head the only thing out of the water, lolling to one side. He appears to be enjoying himself.

"Neigh. *(Take a look at this, Routa. It's amazing, this spring. It's so warm and feels so good.)*"

"Woof. *(Doesn't it? I'm the one who made it, after all.)*"

This guy. While we were fighting the skeleton, he was just lazing around here soaking in the tub.

I'm so jealous. I want to get in, too. I peed in that weird position earlier, so now my fur is all damp and cold.

"Woof, woof. *(Also, quick question. The flames on your tail and mane have gone out. Is that okay?)*"

"Neigh? *(Hmm?)*"

The horse turns his head to take a look before shooting to his feet with a start.

"Wh-whinny?! *(Th-they've gone ouuuut?!)*"

"Woof, woof. *(Calm down, it's looks like they've relit again.)*"

As the horse surfaces from the hot spring, its mane ignites once more. The glugging of the water pouring out of the hole in the horse's stomach is pretty gruesome...

"Wh-whinny?! *(I-I'm on fiiire?!)*"

Even the fire sets him off?

I guess he doesn't understand his own body. I know the feeling.

I also have no idea what this body of mine can do. Or rather, I wish I still didn't know.

"Neigh! *(Oh no! I'm scared!)*"

"Squeak? *(Are you sure this horse doesn't have some weird disease?)*"

"Mew? *(Isn't he just a scaredy-cat?)*"

"Bark? *(What can a ghost do if they're afraid of themself? Kind of makes you question the meaning of existence.)*"

Not just amnesia, but to also be afraid of yourself, that's rough.

"Whinny. *(Ph-phew. That was scary.)*"

It's honestly exhausting trying to deal with this guy.

I feel like I'm going to cry.

"Woof? *(Hey, do you remember the name Nightmare?)*"

"Neigh? *(Not at all. Who's that?)*"

"Woof. *(I'm pretty sure it's your name.)*"

"Neigh... *(Really...? I dunno, that's a rather mean-sounding name... I'd prefer something cuter...)*"

Nightmare gives out a dejected whicker and flap of the lips.

"Bark. *(No, looking at you I think the name fits you to a T.)*"

After all, you look exactly like a bad dream.

Thus, Nightmare.

I'm sure my dreams are going to get worse, which makes me dread heading home and to bed.

I'll just have to snuggle up closer to my lady than normal.

Snuggle up nice and tight. Bury my face in her hair.

"Mrow? *(Well then, how about the name Mare?)*"

"Neigh! *(Mare! That name is super-cute! It's perfect!)*"

Nahura uses her gregarious nature to instantly make friends.

"Squeak. *(More importantly, we still have to decide what to do with him. What do you think, darling? You said we couldn't kill him, so I suppose we'll have to hand him over to the chef.)*"

"Bark? *(I'd love to do that, but I can't present the old man with this undead zombie–looking horse, now can I?)*"

Something like this would no doubt turn even the stouthearted old man's stomach.

No matter how you spin it, he's obviously a monster, and Zenobia will kill him.

"Mrow. *(It'd be nice if he could transform himself like Lady Len to look like a mouse or a human or some other creature.)*"

"Bark? *(That would be a good idea, but there's no way it'd be that easy, right?)*"

Len said it was pretty hard to learn how to transform into her human form, and there's no feasible way for us to teach him transformation magic right now.

"Squee. *(I could do it.)*"

"Arwf?! *(Wait, you could?!)*"

"Squee. *(I can set up the ritual. But choosing and holding the form will depend on his magical power and will.)*"

Well, isn't Len a convenient character.

Okay, let's have Len get a move on with that transformation magic. Then we can bring him before the old man.

"Arwf, arwf. *(So basically you're going to be transformed to look like something else. Are you ready?)*"

"Neigh. *(A-all right, then. I don't really know what's going on, but I can do this!)*"

"Squee. *(Good, then stay still. That'll make this easier.)*"

Len begins to cast the spell from atop my head. As she moves her paws and chants some creepy incantation, a magic circle begins to rise around Mare's feet.

"Whinny… *(I feel so happy right now. My stomach's full, I'm warm, and you're all being so nice to me…)*"

While waiting for Len's spell to be complete, Mare begins reveling in his good fortune.

If food and a bath are all he needs to be happy, I guess that makes him a cheap date.

"B-bark?! *(Hey, you! Why is your body disappearing?!)*"

Now that I take a closer look, Mare's body is steadily turning more see-through.

"Whinny?! *(Huuuh?!)*"

Despite the shock, Mare's body is still disappearing and has begun to float off the ground slightly.

"Wh-whinny…? *(I-I'm—I'm disappearing…?)*"

"Mrow. *(Maybe he's passing over. He cleared all his earthly attachments, and so now he's passing on, or something.)*"

Nahura seems kind of laid-back about this whole situation.

But this is a major problem.

This is our veggie thief. We've got to hand him over to the old man.

"Neigh. *(Thank you, everyone. I can see the light at the end of the tunnel. It was short but blissful.)*"

"Woof! Woof! *(Wait! Hold it! You can't go yet! You can't pass on until we turn you in!)*"

You can't just dine and dash!

"Arwf! Arwf! *(Len! Hurry it up! We gotta change him from a ghost into something else right now!)*"

"S-squeak?! *(Wh-what?! You can't just spring that on me…! Oh well, here we go!)*"

As Len lifts her paws above her head, the magic circle glows ever brighter, completely surrounding the vanishing Mare.

"Squeak! *(Now it's your turn, Mare! Picture your chosen form! Not something that you find terrifying, but see your ideal form in your mind's eye!)*"

"Whinny?! *(Huh? What? My ideal?!)*"

Regardless of Mare's sudden confusion, Len's spell finishes, and the magic circle at Mare's feet flares with sparkling light.

"Okay, something that isn't scary! Something that isn't on fire, that isn't a skeleton, that has amazing fur—"

Then the spell activates.

And that brings us back to the present.

"So you're our culprit, huh?"

Old man James gives Mare a hard stare-down.

"N-neigh… *(Y-yes… I'm sorry…)*"

"And did my vegetables taste good?"

"N-neigh! *(Th-they did! They were delicious! So fresh and juicy! And the flavor was so rich!)*"

Despite the fact that there's no way he understands what's being said, the old man gives a satisfied nod.

"Well, good. I'll start bringing you out some food as well. But that means no more stealing snacks."

"Neigh! *(Right! I'll never do it again!)*"

"Good, good. That's a good horse."

The old man strokes the nose of the whinnying Mare before suddenly taking a tight grip.

"Wh-whinny?! *(H-huh?!)*"

"Well, that's all well and good, but you still have to work off the portion you've already eaten, right?"

The old man's smirk is definitely scarier than any undead nightmare.

† † †

"Wheeze... Wheeze... *(I think I can... I think I can...)*"

I keep trudging along with a heavy pack on my back.

What horrible penance. It's tough; too tough.

So this is the punishment for stealing from the fields.

"Woof, woof?! *(Hey, wait! Why am I doing it?!)*"

I'm not the one who ate the carrots from the field!

That stupid horse over there waiting for me to bring him this stuff is the one who did it!

A big, black horse is casually eating grass over by the road on the far side of a thicket.

Just standing there munching away without a care for all the work someone else is doing on his behalf.

"Arwf. *(Ugh, this is soooo heavy.)*"

The long containers hanging on either side of my body are made of metal and quite heavy.

If I had tried to carry these uphill without my Fenrir body I would have no doubt collapsed.

"Gwa-ha-ha, sorry, Routa. But we can't get the cart up this climb to the well."

The old man has some of the same containers across his shoulders, and he reaches over to give my head a rub.

"Arww! Arww! *(Hey, you think you can make up for this with a quick pet?! This dog isn't that easy to please!)*"

"Squee. *(That's not very persuasive when your tail's wagging like that, darling.)*"

Damn! With all the daily petting, my body's been conditioned to react! Grr! Pet me more!

"Arwf?! *(Speaking of, Len! Why don't you help out?! Why are you enjoying lazing about more than me, when I'm the pet in this situation?!)*"

"Squee. *(What are you expecting such a delicate maiden as myself to do? Physical labor is the husband's duty.)*"

"Delicate maiden"? Says the one who pounded a skeleton into smithereens yesterday.

And I'm not your husband! You keep saying that, but it's never gonna happen.

"Hff, hff. Y-you're so undisciplined. And yet somehow you're the family dog!"

Zenobia, who is also carrying a few of the canisters, complains behind me.

"I-if you want to be the protector of the Faulks family, you should be able to carry ten to twenty of these."

She sounds like she's trying to show me up, but she's doing no better.

"Bark, bark. (*No, I don't want to be a protector. I'm a pet, not a watchdog.*)"

Zenobia trembles back and forth as she climbs. She really looks like she's struggling.

All this has got to weigh at least a ton.

And while her strength goes above and beyond—as always—it looks like even Gorillanobia has met her match.

The old man even told her to give up, but Zenobia, always brimming with self-confidence, said to leave it to her, so I'm doing exactly that.

After a few more minutes struggling down the mountain path, we finally reach a more open road.

"Hey! Welcome back!"

Lady Mary looks up from where she's waiting in the bed of the cart.

She's certainly cute sitting there swinging her feet while she waits, but nothing beats her smile.

"Arwf! (*We made it, my lady!*)"

I rub up against her after she jumps off the cart.

This helps me recover from the hard labor.

"Mew. (*Well done, Routa.*)"

Nahura calls out from where she's sitting with her eyes closed, legs tucked under her.

These two, always slacking off while I'm doing all the work.

"Mew? *(What's that look for? I had the important task of guarding the mistress, and we played and took a nap together.)*"

"Arwf! *(That's called slacking off!)*"

Damn it. That's supposed to be my job.

I feel like all I've been doing lately is working.

Even though my motto is to take it easy.

"Nice job, Routa. You too, Zenobia—thanks for all the hard work."

"Wh-what, you mean this? This was easy."

Your knees are shaking, Zenobia.

"Bark, bark? *(So what are these tubes for, then?)*"

The sturdy metal canisters contain water that was pulled up from the mountain well.

If we came all the way out here to get it, I figure it has to be fairly precious water.

Given how particular the old man gets as a chef, even about water, it stands to reason.

"Mr. James, what's so special about this water that we came to get here today?"

My lady asks my question for me.

"Ahhh, guess I didn't explain. This here is a special type of mineral water."

The old man opens one of the tubs, and the lid comes off with a pop.

"Wha?!"

"Arwf?! *(Whoa, what was that?!)*"

Both my lady and I jump in surprise.

Old man James glances over at us while pouring some of the water into a glass.

I stick my nose close to the glass to take a sniff and peer at the water inside.

It looks just like any other water……

Wait, there are little bubbles rising in it.

Could this be…?

"Hee-hee. Routa, your face looks silly through the glass."

"Arwf? *(Oh, does it? Something like this?)*"

I change my position and give my lady my best sultry model look, but when she sees it warped by the glass she doubles over laughing.

I'm happy to make her happy. I'll add this to my list of gags.

As we fool around, old man James adds various things to the glass of water.

He adds thinly sliced apple pieces, and the bubbles begin swirling around them. After pouring some honey over the top, he gives it a quick stir and hands it to Lady Mary.

"Here you go, little lady."

"Wow, thank you!"

With a glug my lady drinks down the apple-and-honey water.

"Mmm, it's so bubbly…! Delicious…!"

"Arwf, arwf! *(My lady! Share with me!)*"

I lick the water that she pours into her hand.

"Arwf! *(Whoa, it's super-carbonated!)*"

The bubbles are huge and rise to the top very quickly.

Their power gives a pleasant sensation to the inside of my throat.

The refreshing tartness of the apple and the sweetness of the honey imbue the drink with an almost cider-like taste.

It's incredibly delicious.

"This is one of the few places you can get carbonated water. It's somewhat harsh to drink on its own, but it has a lot of uses in cooking. It can help make pancakes fluffier or meats more tender."

Just as I suspected, it's carbonated water.

We must be using these carefully sealed metal tubes so it doesn't leak.

"Our horses have gotten older and their legs weaker, but thanks to our new friend here, I can use this water again."

The old man pats Mare on the neck over where he's eating grass by the road.

"Neigh. *(I'm happy I could be helpful.)*"

"Arwf, arwf. *(Yep, work is a good way to repay favors.)*"

And because it's my role to be loved, it's like I'm always working. So follow my lead.

"Arwf. *(But wow, that's a big cart.)*"

I cast an eye over the cart that Mare's hooked up to.

Sure, Mare's a huge horse, but even with him pulling it, that's still one big cart.

And it isn't the refined type of carriage my lady normally rides in but a rugged cart made to move goods.

Besides a canopy to protect the cargo from rain, there are no adornments.

It's a 100 percent practical cart.

Normally it would take two horses to pull, but Mare pulled it all the way here without issue.

"I used to use this when I'd go shopping in the city. But then the mansion's horses got too old to pull it. I'm glad I serviced it every once in a while. Looks like we'll be able to use it again."

The old man even services the carts and carriages? He really can do anything.

"By the way, you, you're pretty obedient. You seem quite comfortable with pulling this cart—were you kept somewhere before?"

"Whinny? *(Who knows? I can't remember, so I don't know.)*"

Mare gives a blank reply despite being absorbed in eating grass.

"Meh, oh well. I got permission from Gandolf, I mean, the master. Even if you have another master, you can stay with us for now."

"Whinny. *(Oh, heh. Thank you very much.)*"

Mare gives a happy whinny as the old man strokes him from the top of his head to the tip of his nose.

All while chewing grass. He's way too focused on eating.

Speaking of which, the sun's already pretty high in the sky. I'm starving.

As I look to the side, my lady's tummy gives a cute little rumble as well.

We both look up at the old man with expectant eyes, and he gives a wry grin.

"Well then, we can load this stuff up afterward, so how about we take a break for lunch?"

"Arwf! *(Hooray! Lunch! Lunch! I've been waiting all day!)*"

Sandwiches, sandwiches.

An outing always includes the old man's sandwiches. Without fail.

"This way, please, everyone."

While we were carrying the water, Miranda, who came along with Lady Mary, was preparing lunch.

In the shade of a tree she'd put out a mat and a basket holding the sandwiches.

"Woof! Woof! *(I'm going to gobble them up! I've built up an appetite with all that work, and I'm going to devour them!)*"

I bounce over toward the shade.

"Neigh. *(Ah, that looks nice.)*"

You're still shoving grass into your face! How are you still hungry?!

"Mew. *(Harrumph, none for you. This is a reward for those who've been working so hard.)*"

Look who's talking. You just napped on my lady's lap!

"Squee. *(Exactly right. You just need to stay there and watch us.)*"

You, too! You just hung out in my fur the whole time!

Why am I amassing a collection of people even lazier and more gluttonous than I?!

I want to be the laziest pet of them all!

My internal screaming reaches no one.

Finally, time for the lunch I've been waiting for.

Everyone sits on the mat under the tree.

Miranda and old man James said they'd wait until after my lady ate, but Lady Mary said she wanted to eat with everyone, so we're all gathered in a circle.

My lady is so nice. And food really is better when eaten with everyone.

I'm already at my limit. I've been smelling these sandwiches since the beginning, thanks to my superpowered nose, and there's no stopping the drool.

My tail wags in expectation and keeps smacking into Zenobia's cheek, but I take no notice.

"Why, you…"

Zenobia's forehead starts twitching, but I don't take any notice of that, either.

Right now the lunch that's about to start is way more important!

"They're organized by type, so please, everyone, pick whichever you like."

The large basket made from woven willow branches is packed with sandwiches.

Miranda transfers them to plates with a pair of tongs.

"Arwf! *(They look amazing! And aren't there more of them and more different types than usual?!)*"

There are so many different options, for both the colorful breads made with different nuts and veggies and the fillings, that it's hard to tell if any two of them are the same.

"Hey, hey, no need to panic. I made plenty so you wouldn't go eating the young lady's portion."

The old man sits across from me and laughs at my floundering paws.

It seems those extra sandwiches are for me, because I've been eating more and more lately.

"Arwf. *(You're always looking out for me, old man.)*"

But I'm still a growing pup, so it's not my fault I'm always hungry.

Then again, maybe my endless eating is because the old man's food is too tasty!

Although, as someone who was aiming to be a plump, pampered pooch, I was kind of hoping to get wider instead of taller. But no matter how much I eat, I keep growing in proportion.

Four strong limbs. Sharp fangs. Keen eyes and ears.

Yep, I'm definitely a wolf, or actually a Fen Wolf, and really the King of the Fen Wolves.

Damn it. Who gave me this body?! Actually, I know. It was that no-good goddess!

Seems like my dog act is nearing the end of its believability.

I'm going to have to take some immediate countermeasures.

Well, I've dropped some careless hints. It won't be long before someone picks up on them.

"Bark, bark! *(Oh well, I'll cross that bridge when I come to it. But right now, I've got these sandwiches!)*"

"Mew! *(Yep, yep!)*"

"Squeak, squeak. *(Do be sure to get some for me. I don't want that cook to see me.)*"

Because if he sees you, he'll exterminate you. Why on earth did you choose to change into a mouse?

You're the greatest foe of all chefs.

"Squee… *(When you transform, you need to have a really strong image of what you're going to become… It's easiest to change into something that you're familiar with, and back in my cave there was nothing but bats and mice…)*"

Poor little dragon was all alone.

"Arwf… *(I didn't know; I'm sorry…)*"

"Squeak! *(Your apology just makes it worse—stop!)*"

"Arwf, arwf. *(You must have had it hard for a long time. Maybe I can try to be a bit nicer.)*"

"Squeak. *(Well then, hurry up and marry me so we can fill that hole in my heart.)*"

"Arwf. *(Not going to happen.)*"

Putting all that aside, it looks like everyone has a plate now.

That means we can dig in, right?

Among all the different sandwiches, the first that caught my eye was a simple-looking one stuffed with a thick, rolled omelet.

"Woof! *(Looks great! Thanks!)*"

My mouth gapes and I dig in.

The thin sandwich bread has been lightly toasted, giving it a nice, crunchy texture.

My nose fills with savory scent as my teeth pass through the bread and into the waiting omelet.

"Arwf... *(Hwa, oh my God, it's soooo fluffy...)*"

The sweet flavor of the rolled omelet is soft and mellow, and it melts over my tongue.

And the mustard spread over the bread adds a pungent accent to the flavor. I don't think I'll ever get tired of this sweet-and-spicy combo.

"Meowf. *(This fish sandwich is totally delicious.)*"

Looks like Nahura has chosen a salmon-and-caper sandwich.

The acidity of the pickled capers pairs perfectly with the smoked salmon.

"Meow? *(And which appeals to you, Lady Len? How about the sandwich with the fried fish?)*"

Having secured her portion, Nahura is now caringly looking after Len.

In order to keep Len from being seen by the old man, she secretly tears some of her own food into smaller chunks, like we did with the ham way back when, and then uses her levitation magic to slip it to Len, who's hidden in my scruff.

I don't want crumbs in my fur, so eat carefully, okay?

"Squeak... *(Nahura, I would prefer something other than fish, actually...)*"

"Mew...? *(Eh? Oh, then how about the one with sardines and cheese...?)*"

"Squeak! *(That's still fish!)*"

Heh, what happened to that cat who hated mice? Now look how close the two of you are.

It seems that Nahura has chosen another one of her favorites for the next sandwich.

"Mewf! *(The saltiness of the fish with the creamy cheese is to die for!)*"

"Squeak…? *(I mean, it is delicious, but can we please try something else already…?)*"

"Mrow? *(Ummm, well then, how about the sandwich with the fried whitefish?)*"

"Squeak?! *(Are you even listening to what I'm saying?!)*"

Nahura seems mainly interested in the fish sandwiches. She is a cat, after all.

Although I did hear once, back in my old life, that cats originally preferred meat to fish. The whole "cats love fish" thing came later.

Way back when people didn't have a custom of eating meat, and without many protein sources besides fish, cats turned to eating it out of necessity.

Though if you really think about it, Nahura isn't actually a cat. She's a homunculus in the form of a cat.

So I guess she just likes fish.

"Squeak…! *(Accursed cat! Don't look down on me. Or else I'll give you a taste of just how terrifying a dragon can be…!)*"

"Arwf. *(Hey, calm down there, Len. I'll give you some of mine.)*"

I've got to keep Len in check before she jumps out of my fur.

It would be the worst if she were to turn into a dragon here.

Surprisingly, she has quite a sweet tooth. So she'll probably like this rolled omelet sandwich.

I take some food in my mouth, toss it in the air, and let it fall down into my bushy mane.

"Squee, squee! *(Hmph, thank you, darling. I can't believe that I, a proud member of the dragon race, have to sneak about just for food. I wish these humans were more open-minded…… Whaaaaaa?! This is tasty! It's incredibly tasty! Isn't it, darling?! It's delicious!)*"

"Arwf, arwf. *(Really, now? That's nice.)*"

I thought she was about to start complaining, but the taste of the sandwich brought her back to high spirits.

She may be over a thousand years old, but inside she's as fickle as a child, it seems.

I guess that little-girl form she takes when she turns into a human is more than appropriate.

"Woof. *(Now then, time to choose another sandwich.)*

I think I've definitely got to choose something with meat this time.

I've been keeping my eye on a sandwich filled with a thick pork cutlet and what appears to be something deep-fried.

From where it's cut, I can see the inside of the cutlet has a nice pink color, showing that it's perfectly cooked and full of flavor.

I should eat it. I'm going to eat it.

"Neigh! *(Routa! Please! I want to eat some, too!)*"

Mare's whinny comes from where he stands, scraping at the ground, still attached to the cart.

"Arwf. *(Man, I guess that's okay. But only one!)*"

Otherwise there won't be enough for me.

I pick up a corn-and-carrot sandwich and carry it toward Mare.

This should be good for an herbivore like him.

Though he's actually a flaming skeleton zombie, so strictly speaking, he's not a horse.

But he did say he likes carrots, so I think it'll work.

"Are you sharing your food with Mare? You're such a nice dog, Routa."

Hee-hee, Lady Mary is praising me.

She walks over to where I'm standing, in front of Mare.

"Arwf. *(Here you go. You can eat this.)*"

"Wh-whinny. *(Y-you want me to take it from your mouth? That's so embarrassing.)*"

Just shut up. I'm not too thrilled by this, either.

"Arwf. *(If you don't take it I'm dropping it on the ground.)*"

"Neigh! *(Wait, wait, wait, I'll take it! I'll take it!)*"

Mare grabs the sandwich I'm holding for him.

He chews with a weird sideways motion, and then his eyes shoot open.

"Neigh! *(This is sooo good! I—I—I can't believe I'm eating something this delicious...! I'd be fine with ascending now!)*"

"Arwf. *(Don't you dare. You haven't even begun to work yet. You still have to pay the old man back for the food you stole.)*"

"Hee-hee. It's good, isn't it?"

My lady pets Mare's nose.

"Wow, it's so soft and squishy."

Intrigued by the feel of Mare's nose, Lady Mary begins stroking it with abandon.

"Whinny! *(Wow! These pets feel so good! I'm gonna, I'm gonna...!)*"

"Arwf. *(I said no! You can't pass on. Seriously.)*"

And so we made it through another enjoyable lunch together.

The Faulks family has gained another new member, and it seems like things are going to get crazy again.

† † †

The eastern region of Feltbelk Forest.

While it is still under the jurisdiction of Marquis Faulks, there is an unexplored area that humans cannot enter. And within it is a graveyard.

Though no humans should tread upon this land, there are still a number of headstones and graves scattered across this desolate area.

But just how long has this graveyard existed? The numerous gravestones are weathered to the point of crumbling.

A thick, purplish miasma hangs in the graveyard, and not a single plant grows.

The trees beyond the graveyard still show signs of decomposing, but they haven't been affected by the miasma nearly as long.

"My apostle has yet to return..."

The murmur sounds like bones rubbing together.

And at the same time, the miasma begins to thicken.

"I wouldn't think retrieving a runaway horse would be that difficult..."

The listless muttering comes from a figure standing on a bleak hill overlooking the graveyard.

It sounds like an old man talking to himself.

The figure sits upon a stone throne, wrapped in a dark, shadowy cloak, and looks more like a heretical priest than like a king.

The costume itself is terrifying, but the figure wearing it is even more abnormal.

It's large. Far larger than the average human.

Even sitting upon the throne, it would tower over houses.

The staff clenched in its right hand is more like a pillar, and the jewels around its neck are the size of large rocks.

But most horrible is the lack of any flesh on the giant figure.

No skin, no muscles, no organs. Just bones, looking like cracked pottery, peeking out of the robe.

And looking closely at the bones making up its giant form, you see they aren't ordinary bones.

Each bone is made up of countless human bones, and in turn these giant bones form a giant skeleton.

A skeleton made of an amalgam of corpses.

That is the true form of the giant sitting on its secret throne.

If someone present were knowledgeable of the great war of a thousand years ago, the presence of the Lich, the Ruler of the Dead, one of the Demon Lord's army's Five Demon Generals, would cause them to cry out in anguish.

"I cannot believe there would be anyone among the humans able to defeat my apostle. What could have befallen him…?"

The Lich would never imagine that his favored apostle has been smashed to pieces by a dragon tail, and he grips his cup, filled with doubts.

"Oh well. Things never go as easily as you wish them to. It has been over a thousand years since we, the Demon Lord's army, were sealed by the hero. And while we were able to finally break the seal, I am the only one who has awoken… It seems the hero's seal still contains some of its monstrous power…"

Propping an elbow on the throne causes countless bones to rub together.

"Now, let me think. Just what was the name of that hero...? It would not do to forget the name of one's most hated enemy. Perhaps it is the influence of the seal, but those memories are obscured."

The Lich only awoke a few days ago.

An incredibly powerful magic spell went off nearby, weakening the seal for a moment.

The Lich, master of magic and immortality, took advantage of the opportunity to escape the seal, but the action of breaking out left his memories strangely hazy.

"Maybe that's why my Nightmare fled from me. Has it forgotten the face of its creator...?"

Upon seeing the face of the Lich, the Nightmare screamed, "Ahhh! A gh-gh-ghooooost!!" and fled, agitated, westward.

"I immediately sent my apostle after the cursed thing, but perhaps I shall need to commit further soldiers, as they have yet to return. I put so much effort into creating my undead warhorse. And seeing as it is to be a gift to the Demon Lord upon his revival, I cannot allow it get away."

The Lich raises his left hand in a beckoning manner.

As more of the miasma leaks from the hem of his robe, the clouds in the graveyard thicken.

The ground begins to bulge, and countless skeletons begin to climb from their graves.

"Ruler of the dead, you called for us?"

The skeletons kneel before the being on the stone throne.

"My faithful apostles. Head westward and return to me my wayward Nightmare. It may be unfounded, but something may have happened to your brother I sent earlier. Take care on your journey."

"My lord, we are grateful for your concern! We, your invincible spirit warriors, will scatter the fragile humans and return victorious with your warhorse!"

The skeleton troops respond to the order of their lord with the loyalty of old veterans.

The Lich gives a satisfied nod to their statement.

"Ho-ho-ho, the humans will be no match for the likes of you. I shall await your swift return!"

""""*Yes, sir!*"""""

Each gathers its equipment from its grave, and with a military air and the dreadful aura of the undead, the skeleton army sets off to the west.

This was the beginning of the invasion of the undead army.

One would need all the bravery one could muster.

† † †

Thwap. Smash. Crush. Thwomp. Smack.

The sound of a beating tail echoes through the fields at night.

"Wha?!"

"It can't be?!"

"We're invincible?!"

"How can we?!"

"Be defeated?!"

"So easily?!"

Thus goes the invasion.

The ranked skeletons are mercilessly flattened.

"Arwf... *(Well. I figured they'd be coming, but I didn't think there'd be this many of them...)*"

I'm lying on the ground watching the skeletons being completely destroyed.

It's like a game of Whac-A-Mole.

Just when they get restored and stand back up, they get pounded back into the ground. It's a tragicomedy.

"Squee... *('Well' nothing. I'm the one doing all the work here...)*"

Len complains while still smashing the skeletons with the clearly nonmouse tail that belies her mouse form.

"Woof, woof. *(As they say, those who don't work don't eat. This is your chance to show thanks for your life of idleness.)*"

"Mew. *(It's amazing that you can ignore your own faults so brazenly.)*"

"Arwf. *(Yeah, yeah, I know. Hey, Nahura, you do some work as well.)*"

"Mrow. *(I am working. I keep teleporting the fleeing skeletons back to the front of Lady Len.)*"

With a wave of her paw, the reborn skeletons running from Len's tail are instantly teleported back to where the merciless tail then smashes them back into smithereens.

What a dreadful combo attack. Boxed in with nowhere to go.

"Aaarrwf. *(Just try not to damage the old man's fields.)*"

I yawn loudly, then prop my forepaws under my chin.

The first time I saw a skeleton, it surprised me enough that I peed myself, but now it's as boring as an assembly-line job.

But no matter how certain our victory, we must never let our guard down.

"Whinny. *(Oh d-dear. A-are these guys also looking for me?)*"

Mare pops his trembling head out of the nearby stables.

"Arwf. *(Huh? No idea. But if they keep heading in this direction, they'll trample the fields and then get to the mansion.)*"

And I won't allow either to happen.

Anything that threatens my lazy pet life needs to be crushed.

Though I guess Len's the one doing the crushing.

"Whinny. *(Don't be so pathetic, Mare. If you're going to be one of the Faulks family horses, you need to act more dignified.)*"

"Whinny. *(Come now, dear, Mare's just a girl. She can't help it if she's scared.)*"

Elusive and Grace begin to nuzzle the frightened Mare.

"Wh-whinny. *(I-I'm sorry for being a scaredy-cat…)*"

"Whinny. *(That's all right, Mare. If anything ever happens, our family wolf will save us.)*"

"Whinny? *(Really? Routa will protect us?)*"

"Arwf, arwf? *(Oh, no, don't put those expectations on me. I don't know what you expect some pet to do… Also, Mare, you're female?)*"

"Wh-whinny. *(S-seems so. Tee-hee.)*"

Why are you blushing?

I know absolutely nothing about animal sexes, so I guess this is good to know.

But who asked for a tomboy horse?

"Squeak! *(Hey, you nag! Quit flirting with my husband! I'll get you!)*"

As her tail keeps pounding away, Len jabs at Mare with her little fingers.

"Arwf… *(She's not flirting with me, and even if she were, I'm not a furry, so it wouldn't be very effective.)*"

"Squeak. *(That's right. My beloved is wholly devoted to me. I shouldn't accuse you of having an affair. Forgive me, my love.)*"

"Woof. *(Hmm, weird. It feels like we're talking but not communicating.)*"

"Squeak! *(You and I, darling, have transcended the need for mere conversation when it comes to communication!)*"

Nothing can discourage this woman.

In some ways, her tenacity is inspiring.

"Woof. *(Anyway, where do you think these skeletons came from? The forest is patrolled by Garo and the Fen Wolves, so they should notice immediately if anything happens.)*"

It's hard to imagine the crack team of Fen Wolves would run away from something. So why wouldn't they take care of this?

Once we're done here I might have to go investigate a little.

I decide that with a glance over at Len, who is wriggling about making weird noises while smashing skeletons.

Vomit-Beam Party! ...Or So I Thought, but Meat Is Just Too Good!

"Arwooo!! *(My humblest apologies!!)*"

"A-arwf? *(Um, what? What for?)*"

Garo appears in a sliding grovel.

After Len finished grinding the skeletons into a paste with her tail, we came to have a talk with Garo and the Fen Wolves, but as soon as we set foot in the forest, they appeared before us.

"Awoo, awoo...! *(My lord, forgive us...!)*"

Which then led to this apology.

The rest of the Fen Wolves are groveling alongside Garo.

This begging-for-forgiveness pose with the tucked tail is kind of cute.

Dang it. They've got a cuter move than me, and I'm the pet.

"""Awoo, awoo...! *(Forgive us...!)*"""

The Fen Wolves tremble as though afraid, but I have no idea why.

"Woof, woof? *(Again, what for? Just explain what's going on. I don't know what you want forgiveness for.)*"

I sit down in front of them to make them stop groveling.

"Grwl... *(My king, as it happens...)*"

Garo collects herself and begins to explain what's been happening.

"Grwl, grwl. *(Some days ago, the number of monsters began to increase.)*"

"Bark, bark? *(So? Didn't you tell me that they were increasing when we first met?)*"

Back then some natural labyrinth dungeon had appeared, and it was causing monster levels to increase.

"Grw, grwl... *(Indeed, and we've already discovered many more labyrinths. But in our attempts to cope with them, things here have gotten beyond our control...)*"

"Arwf. *(Ah well, I can see how that could happen.)*"

Last time, with just one labyrinth, the monsters started pushing beyond the boundaries of the forest. If many more have popped up, of course the Fen Wolves are going to be busy.

I'm definitely not blaming them for anything.

I know the Fen Wolves are always working hard.

"G-grwl...! *(Th-thank you for your tolerance, my lord...!)*"

"Bark, bark. *(I wonder if that means those skeleton guys came out of one of those labyrinths.)*"

And if they came out after Mare, does that mean Mare is also a labyrinth monster?

"Whinny? *(Really?)*"

No, I've got no idea.

If the person in question doesn't know, then there's no way I would.

Mare, with her head sticking out of the stable and cocked to the side, is the picture of happy-go-lucky.

It'd be easy to forget that she's an undead spirit horse.

"Squeak? *(So then, what are we going to do, beloved?)*"

Len, tail back to normal mouse size, runs up my back and plops down on my head.

"Squee, squee? *(This forest is my darling's domain, isn't it? Are you just going to ignore it?)*"

"Arwf, arwf. *(Hmm, I feel like there's some other trick here, but for now, we'll go deal with those labyrinths.)*"

But from what I remember, all a regular monster has to do is enter the labyrinth to be controlled by it. Garo said it would use enticing scents to deceive, but it just smelled like toilet air fresheners to me.

If you want to tempt me, you'll have to use something that smells at least as nice as Lady Mary to lure me in. My lady smells as sweet and fresh as cherry blossoms in the spring, and it takes just one sniff to make me happy.

So let's hurry up and get this resolved so that I can get right back to her bed, which smells just like her.

"G-grwl! *(A-are you going to be helping us, my lord?)*"

"Arwf. *(Of course I am. You help friends when they're in need.)*"

Though, to be honest, I didn't have friends in my prior life, so I wouldn't actually know anything about that!

Maybe friends aren't actually like that?! Maybe it's just an ideal! Ha-ha-ha!

…Wow, that's depressing. I gotta stop thinking about my last life if all I do is bring up sad stuff.

"Grwl?! *(F-friends?! Forgive me, my lord…! We Fen Wolves are Lord Routa's ever-faithful retainers…!)*"

Right, I want to get along better with these guys, but they keep trying to invade the human lands.

And if I lose their respect, the Fen Wolves will be harder to control, so I guess it's best to keep playing at being their king for the moment.

"Bark. *(Well, let's go take care of things. I want to finish this before dawn breaks.)*"

"Grwl! *(Yes, my lord! I'll show you the way!)*"

"Awoooooo!! *(Mouth Laser Beam!!)*"

The ultimate destruction magic, my vomit beam, pierces the labyrinth from above, causing it to collapse.

"Grwl! *(Splendid, my lord!)*"

Turning my back on the destroyed labyrinth, I walk back over to where Garo and the others were watching.

"Squee. *(You do well at enduring the scent. It would be hard for me to get any closer. You certainly are amazing, my love. Such firm resolve makes me a proud wife.)*"

From her new position atop Garo's head, Len runs her mouth as always, and as always I ignore it.

"Arwf? *(How many are left, Garo? I want to get this over with. I'm counting on you to lead the way.)*"

"Grwl! *(Yes, my lord! The next labyrinth is this way!)*"

We rush off, following Garo through the forest.

"Grwl! *(This way, my lord!)*"

Soon enough, I get a whiff of that air freshener–like smell, and the entrance to the labyrinth appears.

I walk past Garo and the others, who have halted, and stick my head into the entrance of the labyrinth.

I draw a deep breath, and—

"Awoooooo!! *(Mouth Laser Beam!!)*"

After my vomit beam destroys this labyrinth, it'll be back to following Garo.

According to what Garo said, a large number of these have popped up. I can't wait for this assembly-line work to be over.

"L-Lord Routa?"

"Arwf? *(Hmm?)*"

We pass a silver-haired elf as we run through the forest.

It's the oldest of the elves we saved. I guess their village must be somewhere around here.

Which means that if we don't hurry up and destroy these labyrinths, the village they've worked so hard to build might come under attack.

"Bark! Bark! *(Sorry! Super-busy, so we'll have to catch up next time!)*"

I'd love to see how they're doing, but I've got to resolve this problem first.

I'd like to visit during the day, when I can spend more time. Ever since I saved them, the elves sort of revere me, so it's kind of like my own mini harem.

Nothing sexual—they simply fawn over me. Exactly what a pet needs.

We get faster and faster, destroying the labyrinths one after the other.

"Grwl! *(Here's one!)*"

"Awoooooo!! *(Mouth Laser Beam!!)*"

"Grwl! *(Another one!)*"

"Awooooo!! *(Mouth Laser Beam!!)*"

"Grwl! *(And here's one!)*"

"Awoooooo!! *(Mouth Laser Beam!!)*"

"Grw— *(Here—)*"

"Awooo— *(Mouth Laser—)*"

We dash through the forest, making sure each and every labyrinth is destroyed.

"Haah…haah…? *(Was that the last one…?)*"

"Grwl, grwl. *(Correct, this labyrinth you've just destroyed was the final one. Well done, my lord.)*"

Upon hearing Garo's confirmation, I flop over on my back.

"Arwf… *(Ahhh, I'm exhausted… My throat's sore from all that yelling…)*"

"Squee. *(With all the high-level spells you just used, your exhaustion is no doubt due to the absurd amount of magical power you expended. A regular being would exhaust themselves and die after only one shot.)*"

Looking both impressed and amazed, Len leaps onto my belly.

"Arwf, arwf…… *(This extraordinary body of mine sure does come in handy in times like this, but on the other hand, if I weren't Fenrir I wouldn't have to pretend I'm a dog or go through things like this in the first place… No, but if that were the case, I wouldn't have been able to protect my lady from those goblins—wait, but if Zenobia hadn't been suspicious of me, we probably never would have slipped her guard and gone to town…… Hmm……)*"

"Squea? *(Whatever are you muttering about?)*"

"Arwf. *(It's nothing.)*"

I stop thinking about it, as I'm just spinning in circles.

Right now I should just be thinking about how to best protect my pet life.

I'm not going to let anyone get in the way of my lazy-no-good-pup lifestyle.

And as for things like these labyrinths, I'll take them out with a single shot of my vomit beam.

With the job finished, we gather back at our standard cliff top.

"Grwl. *(We thank you, my lord, for helping us take care of our failure of duty.")*

""""GRWL, GRR, GRWL!! *(Thank you, my lord!!)*""""

With the labyrinths now gone, the scattered Fen Wolf pack has regathered.

They all line up before me and bow deeply.

"Arwf. *(Hey, it's fine. Enough of that. Stand up.)*"

Despite me saying this, the postures of the Fen Wolves don't change.

I've got some thank-you gifts for you guys today, so just wait a little longer.

"Arwf. *(Come on, Nahura, where are you? I asked for this ages ago.)*"

"Squea? *(Speaking of, where was she tonight? What was she off doing for you, darling?)*"

"Bark. *(Oh, I just thought it was the right time is all.)*"

"Squeak? *('The right time'? Right time for what?)*"

And just as Len asks her question, the ground begins to glow.

Nahura's teleportation magic.

"Meow. *(Sorry I'm late. There was quite a bit of stuff, so it took a while to get it all together.)*"

A heavy bundle lands with a thump next to Nahura.

"Grwl?! *(Th-this smell?!)*"

The scent is good enough to make Garo unconsciously rise in her position at the head of the pack.

It's a chunk of meat from the giant boar that has been aged and cured with distilled liquor.

It's been two months since we hunted the boar. And a large portion of it has been turned by the skilled hands of the old man into rich, flavorful cured meat.

I may have pilfered little bits here and there before the aging was completed, but tonight, I've taken all of it.

The old man had said it would just get better with age, but it seemed to be at a good enough point to eat, and I thought this the perfect occasion to share it with everyone.

Of course, I only took the portion that had been set aside by the old man for the Fen Wolves.

I'd never take the portion for the people in the mansion without asking.

"Woof, woof! *(Everyone, thank you for your continued hard work in protecting the forest and the mansion! No doubt there's still work to be done in subduing the monsters that came from the labyrinths, so eat this to regain your strength!)*"

The old man's meals are super-tasty, but I think tearing into a chunk of raw meat like this will have more appeal to the Fen Wolves.

Judging by the pack suddenly leaping to their feet, drool pouring and tails wagging, I'd say my assumption was correct.

"Gr-grwl! *(W-wait, everyone! We haven't received our lord's permission yet!)*"

Garo tries her best to keep things in check, but her tail is also wagging nonstop.

It would be cruel to hold them back any longer.

"Bark! *(Go for it!)*"

""""AR-AR-AR-AROOOO!! *(Thank you, my loooooooord!!)*""""

Wow, that's a little scary.

The Fen Wolves bare their fangs and as one leap onto the hunk of meat.

Munch, munch. Crunch, crunch. Chew, chew. Gulp.

They're tearing through meat and bone without a care.

They are wild animals, I guess. I grew up in the city and now only eat the old man's prepared meals.

"Mrow! *(This is very good!)*"

"Squee! Squee! *(It is. This aging, as you called it, is completely different from spoiling. But it's also different from fresh meat still with the blood dripping from it!)*"

Looks like I'm the only civilized one here.

Nahura and Len are both mixed in with the Fen Wolves, digging into the meat.

If that wimpy Mare saw something like this, she'd probably faint dead away.

"Meow? *(Are you not going to have any, Routa? It's delicious!)*"

"Squee. *(It's rare for you to not have an appetite, darling.)*"

I don't want to hear anything about appetites from the likes of you two.

I don't…but if it's that good, I'm also getting a bit interested in trying it.

"Arwf… *(W-well, it's not like I want to try it or anything…)*"

While I'm pretending not to care, it is a little bit lonely to be the only one not eating.

Maybe it's this body, but I'm not feeling any revulsion to raw meat at all. Quite the opposite: The smell is working up my appetite.

"Woof, woof! *(I—I guess I'll give it a try! Make room!)*"

No one can stand in the way of my Fenrir body.

"Arwf arwmf. *(Wow, what the— I figured it wouldn't have much flavor, being raw, but it's crazy tasty. The fat is so sweet, and it has a kind of whiskey finish!)*"

Back in the mansion, we always have the old man's handmade dishes at mealtimes, so I don't really get the opportunity to just taste the ingredients on their own.

This is my chance. I'm going to savor it.

"Munch, munch. Crunch, crunch. *(And these bones are good, too! The bone marrow in particular!)*"

The strong jaws of the Fen Wolves tear through the boar's bones like butter.

We cram the food into our mouths until not a single morsel remains.

"Arwf… *(I'm stuffed… Even the bones being delicious is a new discovery for me.)*"

I wonder if those skeleton guys that Len smashed would have been delicious…

Whoops, I just imagined the flavor.

Shlrrp.

† † †

"Wh-what was that? Was that just a chill…? What in the world would give me, the Ruler of the Dead, the chills…?"

In a far-flung location, waiting for his underlings to return, the Lich feels a chill run through his fleshless bones.

"What could have caused it…? This feels similar to an audience with the Demon Lord…"

It's the same sensation he felt when kneeling in front of the lord of all monsters.

Just like being small, pitiful prey before a larger predator.

"It can't be… Has the Demon Lord been resurrected…?! No, it can't be that. The hero's seal still holds strong. If it were to fall, I am certain I would sense it immediately. So what could have caused that feeling…?"

The Lich glares at the empty sky while suppressing the shaking and rattling of his arms.

"And my soldiers have yet to return… What on earth could be happening out west…?!"

The existence of a mighty presence has given the Lich a great sense of unease.

"This graveyard is an important strategic position for the Demon

Lord's army. I cannot go myself. I suppose I have no option but to send more soldiers... I shall have to postpone retrieval of my Nightmare. And this time their priority will be to return with information..."

With shaking hands, the Lich begins to summon a large number of soldiers from their graves.

All the while unconsciously thinking that such an action is futile.

"Arwf. *(What a beautiful day.)*"

I stick my head out of the carriage to feel the wind.

It's already almost midsummer, so the inside of the carriage is sweltering.

Today we're going back to one of my lady's favorite places, the sacred lake, to cool off.

Though this "sacred" lake is sort of a sham. I don't think it actually has any holy power.

The true protectors of the forest are that group who revitalized themselves at the cured meat party yesterday and are back today to race around the forest and subjugate monsters.

The hardworking Fen Wolves. Never mind me. I leave the peace of the forest to you guys.

I've got important business to attend to. I have to play with Lady Mary today.

"Routa, Routa."

My lady wraps her arms around my neck from behind and gives me a squeeze.

"Arwf, arwf. *(Oh, my lady, you're so daring. Though I am a dog, so it's not really an issue. Feel free to hug me as much as you'd like.)*"

"Mmmmm, Routa, you're so soft."

Aren't I, though? I'm the absolute softest.

And Lady Mary smells so nice, I always like hugging her or being hugged by her. This sort of thing is a win-win. We're the perfect pair of mistress and pet.

"Neigh. *(You two sure do seem close. I'm kind of jealous.)*"

Mare, who's trotting alongside the carriage, pulls her head close to mine.

"Woof, woof! *(No way! Lady Mary is my lady and mine alone! Now leave! Leave!)*"

"Whinny. *(Y-you don't have to say it like that.)*"

With a whinny Mare pulls her head from the window.

Hmph. I'm the only one my lady can hug.

Get outta here. Go on, git.

"Hey, are you thinking about eating my horse...?"

Zenobia questions me with a threatening voice from her position astride Mare.

"Aroooooo?! *(What?! Where did that come from?!)*"

Dang it, Zenobia. Are you really still suspicious that I'm going to attack someone?

Just stop already. You know I'd never even hurt a fly.

And what's with that "my horse" crap? Mare's part of the Faulks family; she's not just yours.

"Strong legs, obedient attitude. Immediate understanding of detailed instructions. You don't often find horses of this quality. You could definitely become a mount of some renown."

Zenobia takes one hand off the reins and gives Mare a gentle pat on the neck.

"Whinny. *(Eh-heh-heh, I'm flattered. This lady's real nice.)*"

Yeah, I guess she is. I'm the only one she ever really attacks.

Please, Zenobia, lay off. I'm begging you, stop treating me like I'm a monster.

Meanwhile, you're riding that horse, who actually *is* a monster.

If that transformation magic wore off, you'd see that she's actually a grotesque zombie horse.

Zenobia's always so suspicious of everything, so why hasn't she noticed that?

I wish she were that oblivious when it comes to me!

"M-my lady, we're almost at the lake, so please have a seat."

The voice of Toa, the little maid, comes from the driver's seat.

She's gripping the reins of the carriage with a slightly nervous expression.

"Whinny? *(Hey now, hey now, are you doubting our surefootedness?)*"

"Neigh. *(Hmm, I'd wager our position in the Faulks family that we'd never cause any choppiness.)*"

"Whinny. *(Ha-ha-ha, of course not. We've been pulling this carriage since the little lady was a baby, after all.)*"

Elusive and Grace, ever the old married couple, laugh back and forth with each other.

These two could probably make the trip to and from the mansion and the lake without a driver, no problem.

That said, it's unexpected to have little Toa there in the driver's seat.

It's hard to see her as anything but the clumsy laundry dropper I've come to know.

Though her dropping the laundry was kind of my fault, since I was the one who surprised her.

"Ohhh, is she all right up there…?"

Miranda, Toa's superior, is fretting to herself while keeping an eye on the driving situation.

I guess she's also in charge of training Toa, and it's got her feeling nervous.

Oh well, even if Toa's nervous, it looks like she's getting used to the reins. But if there's nothing to worry about, it's still probably best to heed her warning.

"Arwf. *(Come on now, my lady, time to get back in your seat.)*"

"Hmph."

Lady Mary shakes her head while her face is still buried in my fur.

With her still latched onto my neck, I pull my head back in from the window.

And soon thereafter we arrive safely at the lake.

† † †

"Take this, and this!"

"Wahhh! Lady Mary, what was that?!"

"Come on, now, Toa, you give it a try. Take this."

"Please don't, my lady!"

Lady Mary and Toa have changed into swimsuits and are playing in the water.

The sight of two young girls innocently playing together is sacred.

"M-my lady, I c-can't swim! Don't make me go into the deep area!"

"Don't worry, I can't swim, either!"

"That doesn't make it better at all!"

Rather than playing *together*, perhaps it's more appropriate to say that Lady Mary is playing *with* Toa—as in "messing with."

Toa, on the verge of tears, is being pulled about by Lady Mary.

There just aren't many others around her age in the mansion, after all.

Toa has been working so hard learning her duties that she hasn't had much time with Lady Mary, but looking after her is also part of the job.

It seems Miranda will still be her primary retainer, but they also thought someone closer in age would be good for her.

And it definitely looks like my lady is having a lot of fun. She's more active and merrier than usual.

That's nice to see.

I swim nearby, but not so close that I'm in the way.

No, I'm definitely not peeping. I'm just watching. Look but don't touch.

"Whoa, my feet can't reach the bottom!"

"E-eek!"

Whoops, looks like it's time to save the day.

I dog-paddle between the two of them and act as their floatie.

"Oh, thank you, Routa."

"Th-thank you…!"

An innocently smiling Lady Mary and a terrified Toa, dripping snot, cling to my fur.

"Woof, woof. *(Don't mention it. It can be dangerous out this far, so I'm taking you two back to the shallows.)*"

For my super Fenrir body, ferrying these two is nothing.

I pull them back toward the shore, where Miranda is waiting, displeased.

"Toa! What part of that was looking after Lady Mary? What would you have done if you both drowned?!"

"M-my apologies, ma'am!"

"There, there, Miss Miranda. Nothing bad happened. Let's settle this…"

For once, Zenobia isn't advocating for violence.

Oh, right. It's probably because she also can't swim.

Based on Zenobia's character type, when Lady Mary went under she should have leaped right in.

That she left it to me to handle tells me that Zenobia probably swims like a rock. Case closed.

"Arwf? *(Isn't that right, Zenobia?)*"

"H-hmph!"

Zenobia turns away from my smirking side-glance in a huff. Ha, bull's-eye.

"Now, my lady, if you spend too long in the water, you'll catch cold. Time to get out to take a break."

Miranda drapes a towel around the shoulders of Lady Mary and Toa and sits them down in the sun.

"I'm going to prepare some hot tea, so please wait here."

"Miranda, please don't scold Toa. It was all my fault…"

"On the contrary, my lady, it is part of a maid's duties to warn her masters against engaging in dangerous activities. We need to ensure that Toa develops into a proper maid for the Faulks family."

Miranda is normally very kind to my lady, but she is unmoved when it comes to anyone doing something wrong.

"Which is why you both will receive a scolding. Prepare yourselves for it after you finish your tea."

Whoops, that spun right back around on Lady Mary.

""O-kay…""

My lady looks despondently after the smirking Miranda.

Poor them—but this is for their development, so I'll just have to watch over them and lick up the tears.

I also don't want to get roped into the scolding myself. (Actual motive.)

I move a little ways from the girls and shake my body to get the water off.

Otherwise I'd soak everyone with the spray.

"Squeak?! *(Wh-what the—?!)*"

My shaking sends Len flying through the air.

"Arwf. *(I got it, I got it… Aaand caught you.)*"

With her back in my scruff, we head over toward the horses cooling themselves in the shade of a tree.

"Squee…? *(What were you thinking…?)*"

"Arwf, arwf. *(I caught you, didn't I? It's your fault for always sleeping on me.)*"

I can't forgive her for being lazier than a pet like me.

"Arwf. *(Hey, guys. Good job earlier. Sorry we keep making a ruckus all night.)*"

It's not a bad thing that the skeletons keep showing up night after night, but it's got to be interfering with the horses' sleep.

"Whinny. *(Don't mention it. You don't need to worry about that at all.)*"

"Neigh. *(He just doesn't want to look uncool in front of Mare, the old silly.)*"

"Whinny. *(There you go again, saying too much… Cripes…)*"

They're just an old married couple. That's something we can all aspire to.

"Squee. *(I hope we can be like them at some point.)*"

"Arwf. *(If you mean as friends, I'm all for it.)*"

"Squeak! *(No! I mean as a couple! I want a family with lots of children!)*"

I don't think that's physically possible.

"Bark? *(Where'd Mare get off to? She's not with you two?)*"

"*Munch, munch, munch? (Huh? What was that? Did someone say something?)*"

Mare's head pops up, her mouth full of grass.

"Arwf... *(Come on, either chew or speak, not both... You really are a glutton, aren't you...?)*"

I'm surrounded by deadbeats.

"Arwf. *(So it seems like there's been no problem with you settling in.)*"

She's been helping the old man pull his cart about, and Zenobia seems to like her.

She's becomes a welcome addition to the family.

...Wait, is Mare becoming a more valued member of the family than I am?

"Neigh. *(I'm just so happy. The food's delicious, and everyone is so nice to me. I don't remember my past, but I can't imagine it was any better than this!)*"

"Whinny. *(Right, forget about the past. You're a member of the Faulks family now. You can stay here as long as you'd like.)*"

"Whinny. *(Yes, and we're so happy to have you here; it's like having a daughter.)*"

"Wh-whinny? *(Y-you're really okay with me being here?)*"

"Whicker. *(Of course we are.)*"

"Whinny. *(Certainly—just think of us as family.)*"

The old couple's kindness causes tears to spill from Mare's eyes.

"Wh-whinny...... *(I-I'm......I'm so......sniff, sniff...... I'm... I'm so...... happy. I'm just so happy......)*"

"Arwf. *(Heh. That's not something to cry about.)*"

If I had fingers I'd have to rub my eyes right about now.

"Squeak! *(Hey, darling!)*"

"Arwf. *(What is it? Don't interrupt this happy scene.)*"

"Squeak. *(Well, her body's becoming transparent. Should we just ignore that?)*"

"Arwf?! *(What?!)*"

Exactly as Len noted, Mare's body is definitely becoming transparent.

"Whinny. *(I truly am so very happy...... Oh, I feel tired all of a sudden. Both my spirit and my body feel so light......)*"

"Bark, bark! *(Sh-she's passing on?! L-Len! Hurry! I don't know if we're going to make it in time!)*"

"Squeak......? *(Oh, for crying out loud, is this girl going to start ascending every time she feels happy......?)*"

And with the ascension force-canceled and a transformation spell applied, we manage to escape without incident.

† † †

It was dusk when we came back from the lake, and by the time we finished dinner, it was already night.

After playing her heart out all day, my lady is fast asleep.

I sneak out of the bed.

"Nggh... Routa... Bad boy..."

Oops, did I wake her?

"You can't eat the fountain...tee-hee..."

Ah, she's just talking in her sleep.

Of course I'm not going to eat the fountain, my lady. Come what may, I'm not going to start eating stones. If I'm going to eat something hard, it's going to be bones. Bones are delicious.

After tucking her back in, I slip from the room.

Everything should be okay, since I've destroyed all the labyrinths, but just in case, I'm gonna survey the fields real quick.

There's always the chance that those skeleton guys didn't come from the labyrinths, but from elsewhere.

They seemed intelligent, and the way they were trying to retrieve Mare makes me think they're following someone's orders, which is out of place for monsters coming from the labyrinths.

And I'm still a bit concerned about what that first skeleton said about a Ruler of the Dead.

I'm sure I remember hearing about someone like that in that fairy tale my lady was reading.

He was one of the Demon Lord's underlings or something. I don't really remember, but I'm almost sure that was written in there somewhere.

"Arwf... *(Oh shoot, this might be dangerous. I don't think I'd be able to handle one of the Demon Lord's underlings...)*"

I'm really hoping I'm mistaken.

"Squee. *(Who cares, even if they are among the Demon Lord's followers? They're no match for you, my darling. You'd be able to defeat a weakling of that caliber with one bite.)*"

Len pops her head out of my fur and snorts.

Oh well, when the moment comes, I'll just let Len deal with it.

She's our mentally weak mouse and our highly destructive dragon. And she's great in a pinch.

Go for it, Len! My happy pet life is on your shoulders!

"*Sniff sniff? (Hmm? What's that delicious smell...?)*"

Just as we are about to leave the mansion, I catch wind of something that smells good.

It's meat. I'm smelling meat.

It's different from the raw meat we ate yesterday. It has the rich aroma of properly cooked meat.

And it's mixed with the faint hint of a sweet liquor.

It suddenly hits me.

"Arwf, arwf! *(This is the sign of a midnight snack!)*"

"Squeak. *(Excuse me, darling. Weren't we going to the fields?)*"

Right, the fields.

We can't just ignore them.

I guess there's only one thing to do.

"Arwf. *(You go ahead.)*"

"S-squeak? *(Wh-what?!)*"

"Arwf. *(It'll be fine. Nahura should already be on her way, so you don't have to be afraid of being there alone.)*"

"Squeak! *(Do you think me some child who can't go to the bathroom alone at night?! That's not the issue here! You, darling, you, you're just—)*"

"Arwf. *(Have fun out there.)*"

I open the window and shake my head, dropping Len outside.

"Squeak! Squeak! *(Darling—! When I get back, you better watch out!)*"

I ignore Len scolding me from where she fell on the grass.

My mind is already consumed with the thought of tracing the source of this smell.

It's entranced me much more than that labyrinth scent.

"Arwf! *(Time to get a midnight snack, woohoooo!)*"

There's only one person who would be drinking at this hour.

"Arwf, arwf! *(Papa! You know you've got gout! If you don't want me snitching to Hecate, you'd better share your snack!)*"

I dash up the stairs and over to Papa's study, where I start barking.

After a little while, the door opens and a face peeks out.

"So you've already sniffed us out, huh? You certainly keep your finger on the pulse of this house, don't you? Or is it your nose on the pulse?"

It's old man James, sporting a wry smile.

In a departure from the norm, he's wearing plain clothes, a black button-down shirt, and it suits him. He's got the top button undone, which gives him a roguish appearance.

"Arwf? *(Huh? You're having a snack, too, old man?)*"

"Oh well, you better come in. Guess it's a rare guys-only party."

As the old man lets me in, I see Papa reclining on the study sofa.

"Hey there, Routa. I figured you'd show up."

Papa, red faced and grinning, lifts his glass in greeting.

"Master, would you like another?"

"Oh, go on, then."

Old man James fills a tall glass with ice before adding a little bit of amber liquor. He then mixes it thoroughly with a cocktail stirrer until the liquor is chilled and tops the glass off with water.

Judging by the fizzing sound, it must be some of the carbonated water we picked up.

Finally, he adds a slice of lemon and then gives it another quick stir.

He's giving off more of a bartender feel than his usual chef presence, or maybe he seems like a veteran host from a club. A definite silver fox.

"A-arwf! *(Hey, isn't that like a highball?! Me too! Make one for me too, old man!)*"

"What, do you want one, too? Just a minute; it'll be easier to drink if I give you a tureen."

The old man makes me a highball as well.

Because he's served it in a tureen, it looks more like a soup, but I don't care. So long as I get to drink it.

"Here you are, sir."

"Ahhh, thank you. And drop the formality, James. Let's talk like we used to."

"...Well, I suppose, since none of the other servants are here... Have it your way, Gandolf. We'll toss formality out the window tonight."

The two clink their glasses together.

What a cool pair of guys. I should take a picture.

I can't lift my glass, so I just stick my head in the bowl without a care.

Gulp, gulp. Phwah.

"Arwf. *(Wow. You don't taste the alcohol at all, just a nice, mellow, refreshing flavor. It's a perfect cocktail, old man.)*"

It's just a simple highball, but the old man's flexing his skills.

"Hey there, make sure you eat the snacks. I don't want you getting sick."

With that, the old man slides a plate in front of me. On it are thin slices of red meat.

"A-arwf...?! *(Th-this fresh color, is this...?!)*"

"It's essentially roast beef—or in this case, roast boar, I suppose. It's finally matured. I made this as a test, so it'll be just us sampling it. Keep it a secret, all right?"

The old man says this with a shushing motion and a charming wink. I think I'm falling for him.

"Oh-ho, this is delicious. Even without any sauce, it's got a really strong flavor."

"When the meat is resting after being cooked, I leave it to sit in a warm broth. Normally you marinate the meat before you cook it, but this way the meat cools as it absorbs the broth. It's just a little trick."

"Omf gromf! *(D-delicious! And how is it so tender? It's still red meat, but it's melting in my mouth!)*"

The old man has a look of childish delight as he explains his methods to us.

"Heh-heh, the trick is that I used the carbonated water you two were just drinking."

"Arwf? *(Huh? You can use carbonated water in cooking?)*"

Actually, I think the old man said something along those lines to me before, but I was too engrossed in my meal at the time to listen.

Using carbonated water in cooking, huh…? For someone like me, who survived on meals from the convenience store in his past life, it's beyond the realm of understanding.

"You want to steep the meat for about thirty minutes before cooking it. The protein in the meat reacts with the acidity of the carbonated water to make the meat tender. Also, soaking the meat in water replenishes the moisture that will be lost while cooking, ensuring the meat is juicy."

"Oh-ho, I don't know all that much about cooking, but you sure do know your stuff, James. I've never met a chef with such a desire to learn nor a chef with half your passion. The king really made a mistake in letting you go."

Ah, so something really did happen that caused the old man to end up here at the mansion. I guess he was once the head chef for the royal family. But now I really want to know what happened.

"Heh, I'll be a chef no matter where I am, so long as there are people who want to eat. I just didn't fit in there at court. I'm enjoying myself a lot more now."

"That's good to hear. I'm glad I lured you out here."

"Well, you really got me out of a tough spot. I thought my goose would be cooked before I ever got to be a chef again."

The old man makes a slicing motion across his throat, and he and Papa burst into laughter.

"Arwf... *(Hey, now...)*"

That's not something to laugh about. Talk about gallows humor.

"Speaking of which, I once had a major incident regarding stolen ingredients."

"Ahhh, you mean at that big shop where you used to apprentice? The one with the owner who was a major pain in the ass?"

"That's the one, I just remembered. You were telling that fatty to lose weight and such before making off with the entire new shipment of meat."

"Yeah, well, they found me out soon enough. If Lady Marianna hadn't stepped in to save me that time, who knows what would have happened?"

The two certainly do seem to have known each other for quite some time. They're very animated as they recall stories that only the two of them know.

"If it weren't for that little mishap, I never would have met my wife."

"That sure does take me back. And little Mary looks more and more like Lady Marianna every year. She's certainly going to be a heartbreaker."

"...*S-sniff,* and then, someday, she's going to become someone's wife, isn't she...?!"

"Hey there, don't start crying. It's still way too early to be talking like that. Have another drink. We've still got the rest of the night ahead of us."

This is the first time I've heard the name Marianna. It sounds like she's Lady Mary's mother, but based on the fact that I've never met her and what they were saying, I can only guess she's passed away.

And with my lady's propensity for loneliness, I'm thinking she might have passed away when Lady Mary was still pretty young.

I'm going to have to give her more snuggles that usual tomorrow. That's all a pet like me can really do.

"...Hmm? James, do you hear anything?"

"What?"

Still sniffling, Papa raises his head.

"It sounded like something being pounded down quite some distance away... Listen, there it was again..."

"I don't hear anything. Maybe you're drunk and hearing things?"

"No, I don't think so. I'm not *that* drunk just yet. I definitely heard something. It went *whack, whack*..."

Yep, Papa's right on the money.

I forgot about the fields.

Sounds like our friends showed up again today.

I guess that's the end of my drinking party. I've got to go finish this before it escalates.

Leaving the two of them to puzzle over the noise, I slip out of the room.

I use my tail to close the door and then leap from the second-story window.

After a running start, I vault over the walls of the mansion and then make a beeline straight for the fields.

The sound of Len's tail thumping the ground gets louder and louder, but as I reach the fields I let out a shout.

"Arwf?! *(H-how many of them are there?!)*"

The moon illuminates countless skeletons.

There's practically an army of them.

"Neeeeeeigh!! *(Ghosts are scary! Ghosts are super-scaaaaaary!!)*"

But you're a ghost yourself.

I pass the stables, where Mare is freaking out, and head toward where Len is fighting the skeletons.

"Squeak! *(You're late, darling! What were you doing?!)*"

Sorry, I was having fun at a guys-only party.

"Mew! *(Ah! I can see the scraps around your mouth, Routa! You were having a midnight snack while we were here working!)*"

"A-arwf! *(W-worry about what's happening here! Over there, over there!)*"

"Meow? *(Hmm?)*"

A skeleton has snuck up behind the befuddled Nahura.

I make it a split second before Nahura is run through with a rusty spear.

Nahura is hidden under me as I protect her from the skeletons' attacks.

The spears break against my hide, and I don't take any damage.

"Arwf! *(It doesn't hurt, but it's still scary as hell!)*"

"Mew. *(Whoa, thanks for that, Routa.)*"

"Squeak?! *(Hey, you, what do you think you're doing with my husband?!)*"

The destroyed weapons go flying before Len's tail smashes into the skeletons a moment later.

But there are still so many of them. It's a slow burner of an assault.

"Squeak!! *(Ughh, this is so irritating!!)*"

Deciding the smashing wasn't doing enough, Len changed to sideswiping with her tail.

The skeletons are destroyed, and it will be a little bit before they're re-formed.

But just look at the size of this army. Are we really going to have the power to defeat all of them?

"Squeak! *(Hmph, it doesn't matter how many of them there are. Weaklings are still weak!)*"

Mounting my head, Len assumes an imposing stance.

"Arwf! *(Phew, look at you go, Len! We can always count on you.)*"

Go for it, Faulks family wrecking ball number one!

Just in case you're wondering, Zenobia is number two.

But she's probably snoring back at the mansion right now.

Sure, she's a former adventurer, but every time we have to wipe out monsters, she's no use at all. Oh well. If she were here, she'd find out that we're all monsters, too, so maybe she should just sleep this one out.

"Squeak?! *(What are you saying?! Aren't you going to help out, darling?!)*"

"Meow! *(Exactly. Come on, just use that super-magic of yours to wipe them out in an instant!)*"

"Arwf! *(Idiots! If I did that, I'd wipe out the fields or the forest or something! It'd tip off everyone in the mansion that we've been fighting out here!)*"

And that would spell the end of my pet life, so why the hell would I do that?

"Arwf! Arwf! *(Just look at Len! She's only fighting with her tail, without reversing the entire transformation! And yet she still has to be careful to not cause a ruckus.)*"

"Squeak, squeak! *(Oh, wait, I forgot! If I revert completely to my dragon form my power will double! Better yet, I can immolate them with my fire spells!)*"

She hasn't been careful at all. She's just spent so long as a mouse that she forgot she was actually a dragon.

"Woof!! *(Whoa! Stop! You'll burn the forest to the ground!!)*"

"GROOOAR! *(Oh well, don't try to stop me, darling! I will cleanse them all in a sea of flame!!)*"

"Woof! Woof! *(Stop! I'm begging you, stop! You're going to destroy my pet life!)*"

As I'm desperately trying to hold back the meathead dragon, a black shadow leaps toward the skeletons.

The shadow tackles one of the skeletons before biting through its skull.

"Aroo! *(Please excuse my lateness, my king!)*"

It's Garo, authority figure of the Fen Wolves.

"Woof! *(Hey, everyone! You came!)*"

"Grwl! *(Of course we did! We rushed to be by your side, my king! We shall not fail you a second time!)*"

The Fen Wolves, comparable to the skeleton horde in number, dive into the clattering ranks.

"Woof! Woof! *(Be careful! Until their magic runs out, these guys just keep regenerating! Don't drop your guard just because you think you've defeated them!)*"

"Grw, grwl! *(Did you hear that, you guys?! The king desires total annihilation! Kill, kill, destroy them all!)*"

......No, I don't think I said anything that disturbing, actually......

""""Ar-ar-arooo! *(Kill! Kill! Kill!)*""""

The wolves howl their war cries and begin to push the skeletons back.

Wow, they're so reliable. So much so that I almost feel like I'm going to wet myself.

Wolves with lips drawn and fangs bared are terrifying.

But I should stop being intimidated by the battle. I've got to check on something.

"Bark, bark! *(Hey, Garo! We definitely destroyed all the labyrinths, right?)*"

I block a scythe on its way down, snapping it against my hide, and Garo takes the opportunity to crush the skull of the skeleton.

"Grwl! *(Yes, without question! And the number of monsters in the forest influenced by their magic is dropping as well!)*"

Which confirms these guys are coming from somewhere else.

That Ruler of the Dead guy—whoever he is—must be controlling them.

"Woof! Woof! *(Okay, everyone! Let's finish these guys off before anyone in the mansion notices!)*"

""""Awroo! *(Yes, sir!)*""""

Even with their expert hunting power, it still takes the Fen Wolves a while, but the skeletons are eventually vanquished.

† † †

"N-Nightmare, you, why won't you return to the Ruler of the Dead...?"

The final skeleton turns to look at the stables and reaches out as its body crumbles.

"Neigh! *(E-eek! I don't know any Ruler of the Dead! P-please don't come any closer!)*"

"GROOOAR!! *(Hmph!!)*"

Len stands in the skeleton's way, blocking it from approaching the frightened Mare, before crushing it with her forelimbs.

"Arwf. *(Aw, we should have kept him alive for questioning.)*"

"GROOOAR. *(We wouldn't get anything out of loyal soldiers like these. And in the unlikely event that he did tell us anything, we'd have no way to confirm if he was telling the truth or not. You can only trust what you see with your own eyes.)*"

Len just said something clever. I don't have a response to that.

"Bark, bark...... *(Yeah, but I would have at least liked to know where these guys are coming from......)*"

"Grw, grwl. *(My lord, it appears that these skeletons are coming from somewhere in the east.)*"

"Arwf? *(You know where they're coming from?)*"

"Grwl. *(Sir, with our Fenris Wolf noses we should be able to track their scent back to their origin.)*"

The assembled wolves bark as one, offering to take care of the tracking.

They really are dependable. They should all look forward to another reward.

"GRAAAR! *(Right, let us go, my darling! Time to destroy the root of this evil!)*"

"Ugh, do I have to?" is what I'd like to say, but Papa already heard something today, despite being drunk, so if another army shows up tomorrow, we're sure to be found out.

If we're going to do it, it has to be today.

"Arwf... *(But still, Ruler of the Dead...? If what that book said is true, he's one of the Demon Lord's generals.)*"

I just keep worrying that we might not stand a chance.

"GARO. *(Hmph, the Demon Lord's underlings are no match for you, darling.)*"

"Grw, grwl. *(I agree with Lady Dragon. None can stand up to you, King Routa.)*"

Ughh, their shining faith in me is painful.

I'm really just a puppy, and inside I'm just a former wage slave.

Where exactly is all this misplaced faith coming from?

Have I ever shown you anything commendable? I'm almost sure I haven't.

But if I don't do something now, that spells the end of my pet life.

"Arwf… *(Oh well, I don't really want to do it, but I guess I have to…)*"

I just want a peaceful, lazy life, so why do I keep getting myself into one mess after another?

It's probably because that airheaded goddess doesn't listen to people.

If I ever see her again, I'm definitely giving her a piece of my mind.

"Grwl! *(Everyone! Our king heads to battle! Form ranks!)*"

""""Ar-ar-aroooo! *(King! King! Use us as you will!)*""""

The two columns of Fen Wolves go ahead of us into the forest.

"Squeak. *(If I were to fly, the people back at the mansion might notice me.)*"

Back in mouse form, Len clambers up my body and takes up a spot on my head.

"Mewl. *(In that case, I'll join you up there.)*"

Nahura jumps up onto my back and curls up.

"Arwf, arwf? *(Do you two ever think about walking for yourselves?)*"

"Squeak. *(We were fighting only moments ago. Let us have a little break. Though I suppose that even if you weren't fighting, darling, you were still watching our backs and guarding the field and the horses from being overrun.)*"

Nope, that was me hanging back out of fear.

You're completely overestimating me.

"Wh-whinny? *(H-hey, guys?)*"

"Arwf? *(What is it?)*"

"Neigh, neigh! *(Why…? Why are you doing all this to protect me? Those ghost guys are only coming here because they're after me…! Maybe I was friends with them or something!)*"

Mare seems pretty stuck on what that last skeleton said.

The skeleton said to *return* to the Ruler of the Dead. Friend or otherwise, it does imply that Mare came from the same place as the skeletons.

"Woof. *(No, things are different now.)*"

"Whinny…? *(How so…?)*"

"Woof, woof. *(You're part of the Faulks family now. Which means you aren't with those guys anymore.)*"

"Squee. *(That's right—we may pick on you, but you're already part of the family. We're not going to abandon you now.)*"

"Mew. *(That goes for me, too.)*"

Len and Nahura join me in reassuring Mare.

"Neigh… *(B-but still…)*"

"Arwf! *(And besides, you still owe us for what you stole from the fields! You still have to work that debt off!)*"

If Mare, who has been saddled with all the hard labor, were to vanish, who knows what the old man would say?

Zenobia would no doubt straight up accuse me of eating her. No doubt about it.

She definitely wouldn't miss that opportunity.

"N-neigh…? *(A-are you sure it's okay for me to stay here…?)*"

In response to Mare's hollow-sounding question, Elusive and Grace nuzzle into her from either side.

"Neigh? *(Isn't it obvious?)*"

"Whinny? *(We're family now, aren't we?)*"

"Wh-whinny… *(G-Gramps… Granny…)*"

Mare squeezes her tear-filled eyes shut before reopening them with renewed determination.

"Whinny! *(Routa! Please let me go along with you!)*"

"Arwf? *(Are you sure? I'm fine with it, but aren't you going to be scared?)*"

Mare's a bigger scaredy-cat than I am. I never thought she'd say something like that.

"Neigh! *(I want to know what I really am! And more than that, I want to stay with you guys! Which means I need to tell this Ruler of the Dead person to stop sending skeletons after me!)*"

"Arwf. *(Okay.)*"

I don't think he'll be the kind of person to listen to us telling him to stop, but if Mare wants to find out what she really is, who am I to tell her no?

Though she did run away once already, so if things start going south, I wonder if she'll take off again.

Oh well. If she does, you can bet I'll be right behind her.

"Arwf? *(Well then, shall we?)*"

"Neigh! *(Let's go!)*"

Following after Garo and the others, we head off toward the eastern part of the forest.

06 We Arrived at the Enemy Stronghold! ...Or So I Thought, but—YUUUM!

Following the skeletons' scent, we plunge deeper into the dark forest.

"Grwl! *(My king, the scent is getting stronger! Our enemy is just ahead!)*"

"Woof, woof? *(Whoa, already? All right, everyone, if the opponent looks way too dangerous, we're gonna run for it, so get ready.)*"

"Grw, grwl! *(Your Majesty! We Fen Wolves are not so weak that we would flee before our enemy! Order us as you will!)*"

Ah, looks like Bal is here, too.

He's running alongside Garo like a watchdog, and he growls a forceful response.

"Arwf... *(Yeah, I'm sure there's only one weakling here...)*"

Hi, my name's Routa. I'm a coward who would like to flee.

My mutters are caught in the wind and aren't heard by the other wolves.

I might secretly wish that they had heard me.

I don't think I have the strength to live up to their expectations.

"Grwl! *(Over there, my king!)*"

As we pop out of the thicket, a regular grassy plain lies ahead of us.

"Gr-grwl...? *(Wh-what...?)*"

It's just a regular meadow. With not a soul in it.

I had psyched myself up, thinking the enemy would be waiting for us. What a letdown.

Is this really the source of the scent? The Fen Wolves are running around confused, noses pressed to the ground, sniffing for the scent.

"Squeak. *(Hmm, there's something peculiar about this place.)*"

Len lets out a puzzled moan.

"Arwf? *(What do you mean, 'peculiar'? It looks completely normal.)*"

"Squee, squee. *(There are signs of something that we can't see. An illusion, perhaps...?)*"

Our opponent is one of the Demon Lord's generals, so he can't be any ordinary foe.

There's a chance the enemy is setting a trap for us. It would be dangerous to stay here for too long.

It might be better to pull back for now.

"Oh my, what took you so long?"

Everyone turns at once toward the unexpected voice.

"Grwl! *(Who's there?! Identify yourself!)*"

Garo growls at a figure standing in the middle of the field wearing a wide-brimmed witch's hat.

"Arwf? *('Identify yourself'? That's Hecate.)*"

She always shows up out of the blue; I'm kind of getting used to it.

Sometimes she's the family doctor, sometimes the wise witch of the forest. But her true form is that of the alcoholic elf Hecate Luluarus.

"Grr...... *(The suspicious witch... Were it not for our king's orders, you'd be dead......)*"

"Arwf. *(Stop it. You live in the same forest—try to get along. C'mon.)*"

"Whimper...... *(Y-yes, sir......)*"

Garo pulls back her fangs, and we head over to Hecate.

"Arwf. *(Hey there, Hecate, I haven't seen you lately. You been busy?)*"

Nahura said Hecate's been cooped up in her workshop recently. Maybe she's done with whatever it was.

"Same as always, eh, Routa? You don't know the meaning of the word *suspicious*, do you? You really are a great catch."

I have no idea what she's trying to say.

Is it really so odd to greet a friend you haven't seen in a while?

I don't understand what I've done that's got her looking so happy.

"Arwf, arwf? *(If you're here, I assume you already know what's going on?)*"

"Oh, I suppose. I figured you'd have trouble somewhere around here, so I was waiting for you."

And again she seems to know everything, almost like she's seen the future.

"Squeak! *(Hey now, stop with the grandstanding. We need to get this done before morning! If you know something, tell us already!)*"

"Don't be impatient. You can't find the place you're looking for because you're not looking deep enough."

Deep. What does she mean by "deep"? Is she trying to say we should be looking underground?

"More precisely, you need to look beyond our dimensional boundaries. If you search normally, you will never find it. Perhaps it might be easier to understand if I say that you're in the right place, but the wrong world."

"Squee... *(Another dimension...? I don't know all that much about that branch of magic. Perhaps that's why I couldn't see through it...)*"

"Mew. *(Miss Len, you always go for the brute force approach, don't you? The magic you've learned seems biased toward attack magic skills.)*"

"S-squeak! *(Wh-what are you saying?! I know other magics, like my transformation magic! That's a high-level spell, to boot!)*"

"M-meow! *(Th-that's some reaction.)*"

Thinking about how weird it is for a cat to be bullied by a mouse, I get back on track and ask for more of an explanation.

"Woof, woof. *(Okay, I understand the alternate-dimension thing. But how do we break through?)*"

"I could cast a spell that would do the trick, but it will take some time."

"Arwf. *(That's no good. We've got to be back before morning.)*"

I don't want my lady to be lonely.

"Well then, we'll have to use force to break through. If we hit the boundary with enough magical power, we'll drag your foe to our realm. And among us, the magical attack with that much power would be..."

At that everyone turns to look at me.

It's gotta be me.

Time for another vomit beam.

"They are late...! Why has no one returned...?!"

The Lich, Ruler of the Dead, is becoming impatient.

Unaware that the trusted skeleton warriors he dispatched have been crushed to dust, he grinds his bony finger against the armrest of his stone throne.

"There is no possible way that *that* many of my soldiers were completely destroyed... That's impossible... Only the Hero is capable of such a feat."

Coming to a sudden realization, the Lich looks up with a shocked expression.

"It cannot be! Has the Hero been reborn?! No. This is not the time to be searching for my Nightmare. I need to move our location before he discovers this graveyard..."

This graveyard is the source of the Lich's power and the resting place of countless skeleton soldiers.

He hid it behind a dimensional barrier as well as underground with the intent that no one would ever find it.

So long as the Lich resides within this graveyard, he has the ability to summon a limitless army of the undead.

This graveyard is a pivotal location for creating soldiers for the coming invasion of the human world. So it must be defended until the Demon Lord is resurrected.

There isn't a moment to lose. The Hero appears to have been reborn, and so this graveyard must be moved before he discovers it.

"I—I must hurry…!"

The Lich raises his staff, but as he begins the ritual to transfer the graveyard's location, a crack splits the gloomy sky.

"Wh-what in the—?"

There is no ritual to invade this realm of the undead. What kind of magical power are they attacking with?

But before the Lich can process this thought, a beam of light bursts from the sky and pierces his giant body.

"Awooooooooooooooooooooooooooooo!! *(Here I cooooooooome!!)*"

At Hecate's instructions, I fire a vomit beam straight down in the middle of the field.

The beam of light punches through the ground, the soil, the bedrock, and then continues on downward past that.

Is this really okay? I know I'm the culprit, but still.

What if it starts spouting a hot spring or lava or something?

I look around to see the field now has a crack in it and light is peeking through.

And with the way the ground's starting to shake a bit, should I really keep firing this thing?

I'm getting worried, but the moment I glance over at Hecate, the ground breaks open with a sound like glass shattering.

"A-arwffff?! *(Wh-whaaaaat?!)*"

The moment I realize the ground has broken out from under me, I am met by the sensation of weightlessness.

Directly under the meadow wasn't earth, but sky.

We all fall into the purple-clouded sky.

"G-grwl—?! *(Wh-what the—?!)*"

"Wh-whinnnnyyy! *(E-eeeek!)*"

"M-mroooooooow?! *(W-we're falling?!)*"

"S-squeeeeeeeak! *(D-darling! Do somethiiiing!)*"

"Arrrrrrrrrrrrrrwf! *(You do something! You're the dragon! You can flyyyyyy!)*"

So is this what parallel worlds are like?

I never thought it would just be a secondary space like this.

We are tossed into the air without a moment to even react, falling head over heels.

And the ground is rushing toward us.

My stomach is clenching, and I feel like I'm about to wet myself.

"All right, everyone, get it together."

Hecate, falling along with us, has one hand holding down her skirt while the other waves her staff.

"A-arwf… *(Wh-whoa…)*"

Everyone's falling speed immediately slows.

Oh, right, levitation magic.

"Squeak… *(Y-you saved us…)*"

"Meow. *(I never doubted you, Mistress.)*"

"Grwwl… *(Tch, to be in debt to a witch. Disgraceful…!)*"

"Whinny! Whinny! *(I don't want to fall! I don't want to faaaaall!)*"

But we've already landed.

Mare's still panicking, even though our feet are on the ground.

"Arwf…? *(So this is our foe's home turf, huh…?)*"

It's an ominous place.

A thick mist hangs in the stagnant air.

A number of tombstones are scattered about the landscape. An unthinkable number of tombstones.

"Arwf… *(Ugh… Something stinks around here…)*"

It smells like a drainage ditch.

An unbearable stench for such a delicate, sheltered pet as myself.

"This would be miasma. It would rot away the lungs of ordinary folk, but you all should be fine. Though with this horrid smell of dead flesh, I truly would prefer not to tarry."

Yeah, no kidding. I don't want to take this stench home with me, or Lady Mary will tell me I smell bad.

"Arwf! *(Okay, everyone! Let's wrap this up and head home!)*"

"Ar-ar-arooo! *(Your wish is our command!)*"

From across the expanse of this endless graveyard come the howling replies of the Fen Wolves.

"...Squeak? *(...And? Where's our enemy?)*"

"...Arwf? *(...Huh?)*"

There's no one here.

Where'd they go?

"Meow. *(Routa, it looks like the hole you carved out is over there.)*"

There's a giant hole bored into the ground where Nahura is pointing.

It looks like it might have been a small hill before a giant beam of light crashed into it and dug out a giant crater.

We form a circle around it and peek inside.

"You don't suppose the enemy leader had the bad fortune to be standing there, do you?"

"Arwf, arwf... *(Ha-ha-ha, not a chance...)*"

There's no way something that crazy could have happened.

No one's luck is that bad...

......right?

But there is no other sign of an enemy in the area. The graveyard is quiet.

"Squeak, squeak! *(Fwa-ha-ha-ha-ha-ha-ha! You destroyed him before he could do anything! You really are the strongest, my darling!)*"

"Grwl...! *(You've done it, my king...!)*"

""""Ar-ar-arooo! *(Our king is the strongest!)*""""

Len leads the pack in cheering our victory.

Sorry, everyone, I think it might be too early to celebrate. I don't think it's going to be that easy.

My warning lights, I mean Fenrir senses, are tingling, telling me that something weird is going on.

And they're pointing right at the center of this massive crater.

"I think this joy may be a little presumptuous."

"Arwf. *(Yep. Thought so.)*"

I hear clattering noises coming from the hole.

The figure runs up the side of the crater and leaps from the top.

"Heh, heh-heh-heh... So you have come here before me... And to have the ability to wipe me out in an instant..."

The figure that appears is a monstrous skeleton.

It looks like the flesh has been stripped from a giant, with a huge skull towering above.

"To destroy my barrier and to make it to this graveyard—I am impressed... But that will be the end of your achievements..."

Skeletal fingers grip a staff, and a robe appears, covering the figure.

Our enemy's revival takes but an instant.

"I am the Lich, Ruler of the Dead. The Apostle of Decay, leader of the undead army! As one of the Five Generals of the Demon Lord's army, I work to sow confusion. Do not think it so easy to defeat—"

"Arooof!! *(First Strike Beam!!)*"

A beam of light smashes the Lich dead-on and obliterates him.

"Arwf. *(That'll do it.)*"

There we go.

"Th-that will do *nothing*...! How dare you attack me while I do my introduction...! Have you no honor? No desire to fight a fair fight...?!"

Nope.

As they say, it's a dog-eat-dog world out there. And I'm a dog. So I'm going to eat you. *Omnomnom.*

That said, this guy sure is tenacious. Not that I thought I had actually won with only that.

I was fairly confident I blew him away completely, but, like last time, the Lich's body is quick to re-form.

"That power so easily penetrates my defensive barriers… It cannot be…the ultimate destruction magic…?! But if you can wield such powerful magics, exactly who in the underworld are you…?!

"Woof! *(I'm a pet!)*"

"A-a pet…? What is a pet doing here…?"

That's what I'd like to know.

I should be lazing about the mansion living the pampered pooch life, but instead I'm here fighting the Demon Lord's army.

"Whatever you are, this is my territory! My domain! No matter how many times you attack, it is impossible to defeat me here in this land!"

Spreading both arms to flaunt his immortal body, the Lich boasts of his victory.

"Regret that you ever set foot within my graveyard!"

The Lich waves his staff, and the ground beneath the graves begins to bulge as an army of the undead begins to rise.

"Arwf?! *(Whoa, so this is where those guys came from?!)*"

Damn, there's a lot of them.

Probably even more than came to attack the fields.

And they won't die until the magic runs out, right?

Which means, seeing as this is their home field, with limitless magical power, they'll keep regenerating forever.

…Shoot, is this checkmate?

"Grwl! Grwl! *(Do not falter! Maintain ranks! Protect the king!)*"

At Garo's command, the wolves take formation and kill the skeletons with a beautiful combination attack, but the skeletons quickly revive.

The agile Fen Wolves skillfully dodge the skeletons' counterattack, but unlike our foe, we'll eventually run out of stamina.

It's only a matter of time before our movement slows and they defeat us. The longer time goes on, the more disadvantaged we'll be.

"GROOOOOAR!! *(Get off of me!! Infuriating creatures!)*"

Len has transformed back to dragon form and is using her entire body to crush the skeletons. But given how many of them there are, her efforts are a drop in the bucket.

"GROOOOOOOAR! *(I'll burn you all at once!)*"

Her fiery breath immolates the skeletons around her, but they just re-form from the ashes. We're just buying time at this point.

"Meow?! *(O-ow! Was that a cinder?! Lady Len, please do that over there!)*"

Nahura, with her nonexistent fighting abilities, is fighting against the flying sparks.

What is she even trying to do...?

"Ho-ho, when you first broke into my kingdom, I wondered about who you might be, but now I see that you have no connection to the Hero..."

The Lich, standing opposite me, mutters to himself in apparent relief.

What's this "Hero" he's talking about?

I mean, there was the one in that book that my lady read to me.

The Legendary Hero Routa, the one with the same name as I.

So if one of the Demon Lord's generals isn't just a fairy tale and actually exists, does that mean that the other generals and the Demon Lord exist as well?

And if so, wouldn't that mean that the Hero this guy is so afraid of could also be in this time?

"Arwf? *(So there should be a Hero, right?)*"

If you exist, Hero, come on out! The guy you're supposed to defeat is right here! Why is a pet like me fighting?!

This is a serious dereliction of duty.

"You are unworthy enemies without the Hero. After you're killed, I shall resurrect you and add you to my undead army!"

No thank you.

I creep away from the Lich and his maniacal laughter.

"N-neigh! *(W-wait!)*"

The cowardly Mare jumps in front of me.

"Well, if it isn't my Nightmare. I did not recognize you in this new form. So you have returned."

"Whinny! *(Please tell me! Who am I?! Why can't I remember anything?!)*"

The Lich stills before Mare's pleas.

After a short moment, his skull begins to shake and rattle.

"Ho-ho, ho-ho-ho-ho. What do you think you're saying? Of course you cannot remember your past. You are merely an evil spirit that I created. A spiritual warhorse that I formed by mixing the ashes of a saint and the bodies of two beasts before laying a curse upon them. That is what you are."

It's as she predicted: Mare used to work with these guys. And it looks like she's a spirit created by the Lich as well.

"Wh-whinny...? *(I-I'm, I'm no one...?)*"

"Unfortunately, after I had finished making you, the Hero sealed us away. It is not that you cannot remember anything, but that there is nothing to remember. Well, I would have figured you would at least remember the face of your creator, but I suppose if you forgot the only thing you ever knew, then making you was not worth the effort."

The Lich puts his hand to Mare's forehead as though grieving.

"Neigh... *(I'm... I'm...)*"

At learning the truth, Mare backs away, flustered.

"You have caused me a lot of anguish, but now you are finally back. Yet with that timid personality, you are not suited to being the Demon Lord's warhorse. I shall have to erase your current memories and plant new ones that will give you a more evil, ferocious personality."

"Wh-whinny...! *(No... I don't want that...! I don't want to forget everyone...!)*"

"Do not be unreasonable. If you want them, I will be adding them to my army after I deal with them here."

A giant, bony hand reaches out to capture Mare.

"Whinny...! *(I don't...!)*"

My destructive magic blows apart the arm reaching for Mare.

"...You have yet to give up?"

The destroyed arm repairs itself in an instant, and the Lich glares at me with eyeless sockets.

Whoa, I think that pissed him off. That's super-scary. I think I'm gonna wet myself.

But I'm still going to say what I have to say.

"Arwf, arwf. *(That had nothing to do with giving up or not. Mare's our family. And if you think you can just take her, then we've got a problem.)*"

"Were you not listening? That horse was originally part of the Demon Lord's army. It is a tool that I created and gave life to. It is different from a monster like yourself. And yet you claim it to be family?"

"Woof. *(That's right.)*"

I think of everyone here with me as family in some way or another.

And it looks like we're all still standing.

You say that Mare is actually supposed to be the Demon Lord's horse? So what?

"Why do you refuse to give up my Nightmare? Are you looking for battle strength? Do you want to take over this world in the place of the Demon Lord?"

"Arwf. *(Ha, you're thinking way too small. You think shallow ambition like that would satisfy me? Okay, I'll tell you. Listen up. What I want is—)*"

Cutting off my words, I draw in the largest breath I can.

"AWOOOOOOOOOOOOOOOOO!! *(I want to eat and sleep and not work and be loved every day and in order for that I need Mare because she's essential to doing all the heavy lifting around the house in place of meeeeeeeeeeee!!)*"

Phew, feels good to get that out.

The Lich is swallowed by a wave of light.

But then immediately starts to revive—again.

"Wh-which is the more shallow ambition?! You desire my finest creation just to make it your pack horse?! Surely you jest! I am appalled by your complete lack of ambition!!"

Rude.

That's my greatest desire.

Without Mare, my happy-go-lucky pet life is going to face some serious hardships.

Not to mention how sad old man James will be if she disappears, and Zenobia, and Lady Mary, and Elusive and Grace, and everyone else at the mansion.

I'd rather not have that heavy rain cloud hanging over my pampered pooch life, thanks.

"Arwf, arwf! *(What I'm saying is, Mare! Don't give up! Let's defeat this skeleton guy and go home! It's time to make your choice!)*"

"N-neigh... *(R-Routa...)*"

"Your positivity is wonderful, but haven't you forgotten something? Your magic cannot defeat me...!"

The Lich, who has finished regenerating, renews his attack.

"Awooooooo! Awoooooooo! *(I'll just keep on attacking! Mouth beam! Mouth beam!)*"

"Ho-ho-ho, it is pointless, pointless! My magic is limitless here. Even with the ultimate destructive magic, you cannot destroy me!"

The back-and-forth struggle between destruction and rebirth collapses, and the Lich suddenly manages to grab ahold of me.

"Arwfgh...! *(Urk, wait, time out...!)*"

It doesn't do any damage, but I can't budge even an inch. He's seriously strong for being nothing but bones.

The Lich lifts me up, suspending me in midair.

Now what do I do? Stuck like this, I can't move anything but my head.

I wonder if he'd accept my surrender at this point.

"You seem troubled, Routa."

Hecate's voice comes from somewhere below me.

Even in a pinch like this, she still doesn't lose her cool.

While I, on the other hand, am freaking out. I'm already starting to pee a little.

"Arwf! Arwf! *(Yeah, just a bit! Or maybe a lot! We're kind of running out of options here!)*"

You got any good ideas? I'd like an amazing plan to defeat this guy, please.

"Well then, how about I give you a hint."

Hecate lifts her index finger like she's giving a lecture.

"Routa, did you enjoy that boar you ate yesterday?"

"Arwf?! *(What?!)*"

It was delicious. Raw, to be sure, but delicious nonetheless.

But what does that have to do with this situation?

"And did you leave any leftovers?"

"Arwf— *(No, we ate it all! Every last bite! To the last delicious bone—)*"

Bone?

Oh, right, we ate the bones.

And these guys are made of bones.

The boar bones were delicious.

Which means these guys, who are made of bones, should also be delicious.

The science checks out.

"And if they're inside the stomach of the strong-bodied Fen Wolves, their magic should be nullified. And without magic, they can't regenerate."

You don't need to spell it out, Hecate. I got it.

"Just what are you talking about? It is no use trying anything. I shall crush you in my grasp—"

I cut the Lich short by opening wide and eating one of his fingers.

"Gwa?!"

Whether from pain or from a burgeoning sense of something being off, the Lich drops me.

Back on the ground, I crunch through my bite.

"*Crunch munch crunch!! (The texture, this explosive flavor... This guy...is delicious!!)*"

"What?! Y-you ate me...?!"

The Lich stares at his hand with shock.

The finger isn't regenerating.

Looks like Hecate was right on the money.

"Woof! Woof! Woof! *(Hey, everyone! I figured out how to defeat these guys! It's easy! Just eat them! Like we're always doing! Easy, right?!)*"

And after all this fighting, we should all be starving.

These guys aren't our enemies.

They're our food.

At my words, the eyes of the Fen Wolves light up.

""""*Drool? (Food?)*""""

The emotionless skeletons feel their first inklings of fear.

Exactly. Look at you all, spread out before us.

It's a feast, isn't it?

Faced with the likes of us, our prey can only say one thing.

"D-do not come any closer...! Stay away...!"

We slowly stalk the skeletons and encircle them.

And then our mouths open wide.

"Grrrruff!! *(It's dinner tiiiiiiiiiiiime!!)*"

""""Awoooooo!! *(Dinnerrrrrrrrrrr!!)*""""

"N-noooooooooooooooooooooooo!!"

The tide turns in an instant.

With me at the head of the pack, the Fen Wolves dive into the skeleton forces and begin devouring their bones.

Snap, snap. Crunch munch. Gulp.

Man, these magic-steeped bones are something else. It's kind of surprising.

The first bite has this kind of musty, stale flavor, but then they turn completely irresistible.

And now for a quick report on the food situation. Everyone's stomach is distended, the skeleton soldiers are completely destroyed, and the Lich, the source of their magic, has only half his skull remaining.

"This cannot be… How can such a ridiculous fighting method defeat one such as myself…?!"

"Arwf. *(You all were delicious. Thanks for that.)*"

My thanks are the tipping point for the Lich's rage.

And yet his powers refuse to manifest, his magic disperses, and what remains of his skull begins to crumble.

"Arwf, arwf? *(Probably pointless to ask now, but just who are you guys? I figured you were just fairy-tale characters, but here you are, so does that mean there's actually a Demon Lord as well?)*"

He said something about a Hero, and I'd really like to avoid more disturbances back home.

So along those lines, how about we just leave me out of whatever's going on?

"Ho-ho-ho-ho, you were after my Nightmare, were you not? And you're sure you want to waste your time asking a question such as that?"

"Arwf? *(Huh? If you're talking about Mare, she's still here. And don't worry, we'll be taking her back home with us.)*"

"Ho-ho, with my power I can command any of the undead. And that includes that Nightmare… If I am to be defeated, I shall be taking it with me…!"

"Squeak?! *(What did you just say…?!)*"

"Mew?! *(He can't…?!)*"

Spinning around, we see Mare's body start to disappear.

"Ho-ho-ho, to cause you anguish satisfies me…! I shall see you on the other side, Nightmare…!"

And with these final words, what remains of the Lich crumbles away.

Leaving behind a dead silence and a fading Mare.

"Neigh… *(It looks like I'm fading away again…)*"

Mare sounds sad but content.

"Whinny... *(Everyone, our time together may have been short, but thank you for looking out for me...)*"

She bobs her head up and down in a facsimile of a bow.

"Neigh whinny... *(And everyone at the mansion was so kind to me... Grandpa Elusive and Granny Grace took me in as family... I've never had a father or a mother, but it felt so warm and loving... It must have been what having a father and a mother is like... I'll never get to see them again, but will you please let them know just how happy they made me...?)*"

Mare's body is almost completely see-through by this point.

She looks at me, tears falling from her eyes.

Of course, for such a wish, I—

"Arwf. *(Um, nope.)*"

I already have an answer.

"Whinny?! *(Wh-what?!)*"

"Arwf, arwf. *(No way... What do you think you're doing, disappearing like that? Didn't I already tell you? You still have to pay us back for the food you stole.)*"

"Whinny... *(But I'm—I'm about to disappear...)*"

Yeah, only if we let you go.

Now, if only there were some other source of magical power to keep your body preserved.

"Arwf! *(Speaking of which, if you would, Hecate!)*"

"Well, I figured you'd ask."

Hecate lets out a seemingly troubled sigh, but it looks like she's got it covered.

"We should be able to fix this by reconnecting the severed source of magical power to Routa. Routa's store of magical power should be about equivalent to this graveyard, after all."

"Arwf! *(You're amazing! I knew we could count on you, Hecate!)*"

Can I give you a lick to show my thanks?

I'd be glad to just lick your feet.

Even until they get pruney.

"Okay then, here I go."

With a wave of Hecate's staff, Mare stops vanishing.

"Arwf. *(It kind of feels like there's some weird pull, but also not.)*"

It's like a part of my magic power that I'm not really conscious of is being pulled out of me.

And as if time were being rewound, Mare's body starts to revert to how it was before.

"Wh-whinny...! *(I—I can feel Routa's warmth filling me up inside...!)*"

Can you please not say it like that?

You've got a nice voice, but you're still a horse, and that's *really* not my thing.

Back to how she was before, Mare lets out an excited whinny.

"Whinny! *(Routa, thank you! I really didn't want to disappear! I wanted to stay here with everyone!)*"

"Bark! *(Well, that's good to hear. So keep on working hard for the family, okay?)*"

Which, in turn, will let me rest.

A perfect solution where everybody wins.

"Well then, I still have things that need attending to, so I'll be leaving first."

As she speaks, the ground lights up around Hecate. Teleportation magic.

"Arwf? *(Hmm? You still have work to do?)*"

"Magical disasters—have you forgotten?"

"Arwf... *(Ah...)*"

Oh, right. Whenever we cast too many spells in one location, that magical power builds up, and unless addressed, it can give birth to new monsters or disasters.

And this time we've got the bonus of all this miasma hanging about. If we don't take care of it, the guild will send investigators again.

And I don't want to deal with that hassle a second time.

Which is why it looks like Hecate is going to seal it all up once more.

"Arwf, arwf. *(Sorry about all this, Hecate.)*"

"Don't worry about it. I'll merely take some of Gandolf's liquor as payment."

"A-arwf. *(S-sure. Just be gentle, please.)*"

Sorry, Papa. I can't stop her.

I'm giving up your treasured alcohol to protect my pet life.

As the gleam from the ground grows in strength, the air between us and Hecate glows a blinding white.

"...That's two down. Four to go... And then little Mary will be—"

Hecate mutters something as she lifts her staff, and we all vanish through her teleportation magic.

The next morning, we split ways in the forest, and I head back to the mansion.

Where—

"Routa, you stink! Just where have you been playing?!"

"*Whimper. (Hrmmm. My lady, please don't run away! Don't hate me!)*"

After Hecate transported us back with her teleportation magic, I washed myself off in the fountain, but it seems like I didn't get all the smell off.

The stench of the graveyard is embedded in my fur.

When my lady woke up this morning and realized I wasn't there, she tracked me down and jumped me, burying her face in my chest. A moment later she stiffened up, and this happened.

"*Hnnnnh! (I-it's not BO! It'll come off if I wash myself properly! I'll wash better and it'll come right off! Don't get rid of me, my lady!)*"

"Bath! Right now! And until you get nice and clean in the bath, there will be no snuggles!"

Does it really smell that bad? My lady is hiding around a corner down the hall and refuses to come any closer.

She's got a menacing look with her cheeks puffed out.

She's super-cute like this. I want to rub up against her.

But if I were to do that now, she'd just get even more angry with me, so I'd better be a good boy and head to the bath.

"A-arwf… *(F-farewell, my lady, until we meet again…)*"

With hands pinching noses, the maids lead me like a lamb to slaughter toward the bath, where I am thoroughly cleansed.

† † †

"Arwf? *(Hey there, Mare, Elusive, Grace, how're you all doing?)*"

Thoroughly scrubbed down to the bone, I was kicked out of the bathroom by the maids with a "And don't you come back!" After my fur dried, I headed out to the stables.

Even with our midnight battles, it doesn't look like there's any damage to the nearby fields.

Oh, the old man's out inspecting those very fields.

He's muttering about something, but it's probably only that thing where people talk to their vegetables.

"Neigh! *(I feel great! Thanks to your magic, Routa, I'm feeling much better than before!)*"

Nice, very nice. Repay my magic loan with lots of hard work.

Ever since Mare showed up, the old man's been giving me fewer and fewer chores.

Which has led to me being able to double my nap time.

"Neigh. *(Thank you, Routa.)*"

"Whinny. *(Thank you for bringing us such a wonderful little girl. Thank you so much. Ever since you've arrived, this mansion has had nothing but good tidings.)*"

Yeah, I wonder about that.

Sometimes it feels like I've brought nothing but trouble.

"Whicker. *(The mistress is so much healthier, and Mr. James seems to have found a new zest for his work. Everyone in the mansion seems so much brighter, and there's no mistaking that it's all thanks to you.)*"

Aw geez, you going on like that is making me bashful.

I'd say I'm the one who was saved. Taking on the role of pet has done wonders for me.

"…Wh-what the heck is thiiiiiiiiiiiiiiiis?!"

Whoa, what's going on?!

The old man's yell suddenly rings out from the fields.

"Arwf, arwf? *(Hey, old man, what is it?)*"

I run over to where he's fallen backward.

"M-m-my vegetables… My vegetables…!"

"Arwf? *(The vegetables?)*"

I follow his gaze.

And there—

"Arwffff! *(They're huuuuuuuuge!)*"

The tops of massive carrots are popping up out of the ground.

But not just carrots. All the vegetables surrounding the carrot patch are giant.

"Squee. *(Those look big enough to feed us for a long while.)*"

To avoid being seen by the old man, Len's murmuring from her position tucked away in my fur.

"Arwf, arwf. *(Now, let's not get carried away. But still, what's with this size?)*"

They're too big for the old man to pull with both hands. They've got to be a couple hundred kilos at least.

"Squee? *(Well, it's got to be that, right?)*"

And exactly what is *that*?

Seems like Len has some idea as to what's happened.

"Squeak, squeak? *(Darling, isn't this around where you urinated?)*"

The first time I saw one of those grim reaper–looking skeletons, I guess I did pee myself a little bit out of surprise.

And then Len shattered the skeleton with her tail.

"Squeak. *(Well, that would be it. It looks like Fenrir urine mixed with undead bone dust makes for good fertilizer for the fields.)*"

Huh? My piss has that much of an effect?

…Do you think it's okay to eat these?

"Squeak, squeak… *(They're certainly unusual, but they shouldn't cause any harm. Rather, they should be packed with nutrients and do nothing but good for the body. It could probably even be classified as a magical medicine. Were we to take them to market, they would no doubt command a hefty sum...)"*

For real? I just unknowingly created a new magic item.

"Squeak. *(My urine has a similar effect. The grasses you took when you came to my lair are quite similar.)*"

Ah, the wonder drug that I needed to save my lady.

The wyrmnil, I believe it was called.

The precious magical medicine that could never be found in the marketplace.

And yet was growing all over Len's lair.

A veritable field of shining wyrmnil, growing at the end of the cave.

"Squeak. *(Yes, yes, exactly. It grows all over my toilet area. I thought it strange that you wanted such a thing.)*"

...What? Toilet?

Did you just say toilet?!

"W-woof! Woof?!! *(Wh-what did you make my lady drink?!!)*"

"Squeak?! *(Wh-what?! Isn't it thanks to that herb that she's doing better?! You should be thanking me instead of yelling at me! You can't find another magical herb that compares to grass watered with dragon urine! Maybe you want to try drinking it directly?!)*"

"Woof! Woof *(Shut up already! Wyrmnil?! More like Urinil!)*"

After all, wyrmnil is an extract of the magical properties of dragon urine.

Heh, what a name. I'll have to introduce whoever named wyrmnil to one of my vomit beams.

"Whinny! *(Carrots! Carrots! Look at them!)*"

At least Mare is excited.

With this much, I can imagine a fair amount will be going to her and the other horses.

But still, what's the old man going to do with these giant vegetables?

"Heh, heh-heh-heh. Are these meant to challenge me?"

Whoops, looks like he's getting excited, too.

"I've no lack of subjects to test new recipes on! You guys! I'm leaving the poison checking to you!"

Poison checking?! Not sampling?!

Sure, the ingredients are strange, but still!

Oh well, not even the undead could upset my stomach, and they were in fact pretty tasty.

And I wouldn't want my lady to be served anything that might be dangerous, after all.

Okay then, bring it on!

"Whinny! *(Me, too! I'll test, too! Please!)*"

We ate a lot of vegetable dishes after that.

Afterword

Hello, good evening, and good night, this is Inumajin.

Thank you so much for buying the third volume! I'm so glad to see you all again!

I'd like to start off by introducing you all to an easy recipe that appears in the story! What? Of course I'm not running out of material to use for the afterword. *Mutter mutter.*

Today we're looking at the garlic toast with fatty roast pork that was served in the pub.

I say "toast," but it's actually a type of food from Italy that's called bruschetta. It's a simple dish, with ingredients like meat or vegetables piled on thinly sliced bread, but with so many practical uses, it's the perfect snack or party food.

What you might have found unusual in the story was the cured, salted pork fat.

I wrote it as cured, salted back fat, but it's actually a processed food called Lardo, made by curing pork fat in salt and herbs and then smoking it. It's the local specialty of the Italian town Colonnata.

The outside is thoroughly rubbed with spices, and it tastes just like cured ham.

It has a little quirk whereby the part closest to the skin usually has a bit of a crunchy texture, while the part closest to the meat is so soft it almost melts. It's incredibly delicious. It's great on its own, but when it's served over bread or pasta, the fat gets warm and melty, and it's so tasty it's almost unbearable.

You can find it in a lot of supermarkets in the foreign foods section, so please search for it.

Now I'll give the ingredients and explain how to prepare it.

Ingredients: French bread, olive oil, roasted garlic (in a bottle in the spices section), Lardo (you can buy it in chunks, but it can be difficult to slice, so it's easier to buy packs of thin slices).

Preparation: Slice the French bread into thin slices and heat in a toaster until just before it turns brown. Add a splash of olive oil to the baked bread. Rub the roast garlic deep into the bread. Top with thin-sliced Lardo. And complete.

Huh? That's not enough? That's fine! Simple and delicious is the best!

If you're looking to take it one step further, I'd recommend topping the Lardo with rosemary and pink pepper to give it a boost in appearance and flavor. With just this one little step, you can make people think it's a much more elaborate dish. Seriously. It'll trick them. (I'm onto you, chefs.)

Anyway, that's enough for today. See you all again in the fourth volume!

2018.5 Inumajin

CRUNCH! NOM! MUNCH!

Crackle! Nibble! Gnaw!

Munch! Crunch! Gulp!

Man, the food sure is good today!

It is indeed delicious, but aren't you eating a little too much, darling?

You're definitely bigger than you were last month. Eventually, you won't even be able to fit in the mansion anymore.

Is that so? Well, that sounds like a problem for future Routa! Oh, Lady Mary is calling me! I'm coming! Just a sec! ...Urgh?!

What's the matter, beloved? Why did you stop in the doorway?

...I-I'm stuck... If I try to move, I'm gonna break the doorframe...

I told you so...

Routa's finally too big to fit through the door!
If he wants to continue living his pampered pooch life, he'll have to get serious!
Next Volume: I'm going on a diet! ...Or so I thought, but...

Woof Woof Story Vol. 4 Coming in 2020!

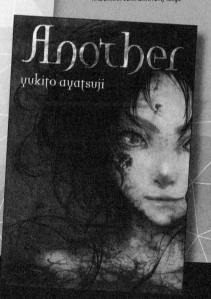